Praise for Jason Phillip Reeser's

Cities of the Dead

"Jason Phillip Reeser proves an expert guide to the necropoli of New Orleans, where some of his thirteen tales from these moldering crypts pay homage to the classic pulp magazines. Others, however, engage deeper philosophical questions of morality and mortality, as the dead try unsuccessfully to make their peace with one another and with the living, who are equally incapable of breaking through the time-worn yet timeless marble that separates two levels of being. As one hapless soul concludes, 'Death was not going to be terribly different from life.' "

R.S.Gwynn,
University Professor, Lamar University
Author of *The Narcissiad* and *The Drive-In*

"Given how lively and rich the characters are in Jason Phillip Reeser's debut collection, it seems terribly ironic that they are mostly dead. Even in death though, they yearn for what we yearn for—happiness, freedom from fear, understanding, love, some meager dream of hope or salvation. That such things elude them still is part of what makes *Cities of the Dead* so powerful and compelling. Floating from story to story, I felt like a man gawking at headstones, and after finishing the book, I felt haunted by truths I couldn't name, as I do after a visit to a graveyard."

Neil Connelly,
Assistant Professor of English, Shippensburg University
Author of *St. Michael's Scales, The Miracle Stealer*

"Like Emily Dickinson, Jason Phillip Reeser is intrigued by the theme of consciousness after death. Like Edgar Allan Poe, he knows that a guilty conscience can produce hells that are worse than Hell. And like Rod Serling in the old *Twilight Zone* TV series, he knows how to present little paranormal vignettes that leave his audience wondering. Put it all together with a twist of Louisiana Gothic and you have a recipe for an enjoyable read."

Julie Kane
Poet Laureate of Louisiana
Professor of English, Northwestern State Univ. of Louisiana
Author of *Jazz Funeral*,
2009 Donald Justice Poetry Prize winner

"In the current literary undertow, where desultory chatter poses as drama and self-regard becomes both an ersatz setting and an even more dispiriting temperament, Jason Phillip Reeser's *Cities of the Dead* is a curative for these impoverished contours.

"The language of each tale is unembellished yet fills the page with local color, universal emotion, and an un-ironic romance for the deathly that lurks throughout so much of life itself. Where dull minds often see "a melting pool of smoke and terror," Jason bears witness to a panoptical *joie de mort*, guiding us beside unfamiliar voices and telling inscriptions to an intimacy with the ethereal.

"Three works from this collection have already graced the pages of *Danse Macabre*. We're jealous we didn't get all the others. But in *Cities of the Dead*, connoisseurs of bespoke story-telling get the panoply of Jason's macabre quill. Little gods may die, but good *erzählungen* are forever."

Adam Henry Carrière
Editor/Publisher of
Danse Macabre An Online Literary Magazine™

Other books by Jason Phillip Reeser

Jury Rig

The Lazaretto

Cities of the Dead

A collection of short stories by
Jason Phillip Reeser

ISBN:978-0615703862

Cover art by Kathryn Reeser
Copyright ©2012 by Kathryn Reeser

Saint James Infirmary Books
Westlake, Louisiana
editor@saintjamesinfirmarybooks.com

For Jennifer—
Thank you for teaching me about
life and death, and always
insisting that each story
was better than the last.
I love you.

Saint James
Infirmary
Books

"The Wanting Dead" appeared in *The Louisiana Review*.

"What Scares Henry Payne", "The Rossi", "The Prophet", and "The Unbroken Seal" appeared in *Danse Macabre Magazine*.

The author gratefully acknowledges the editors for their generosity.

Table of Contents

The Wanting Dead.. 1

Resurrection...17

The Imposter 32

The Unbroken Seal 45

The Soldiers' Home 58

What Scares Henry Payne..71

The Dream Monger 86

The Rossi 98

A Night in the City of the Dead.................................. 117

Come Out, My Love 133

Mugging the Dead...146

Grave Robber 164

The Prophet 181

When they talk of ghosts of the dead who wander in the night with things still undone in life, they approximate my subjective experience of this life.

--Jack Henry Abbot

An idea, like a ghost, must be spoken to a little before it will explain itself.

--Charles Dickens

And all wept, and bewailed her: but he said, Weep not; she is not dead, but sleepeth.

--Luke 8:52 KJV

The Wanting Dead

(*The Louisiana Review*, Spring 2008)

My first night in the City of the Dead was a real eye-opener. I was not in the least ready for anything that happened. But then, no one alive can prepare you for your first night as one of the dead. No one really tries. And why should they? I would never have listened. I never listened to anyone when I was alive. I had no idea I would learn to listen so well once I was dead. But death is full of so many surprises.

I'd like to explain how it all came about. At least how the night progressed. It is a curiosity I'd like to be able to describe logically—how I was lying in the coffin, surrounded by darkness, and how later I came to be standing outside my crypt, reading the inscription on the faceplate as if I were looking for errors in the nonerasable marble. I remember that distinctly. I remember reading over it hoping I might find some mistake I could point to and say "There, you see? They placed the comma in the wrong spot, so obviously I'm not dead. I may only be alive by a technicality, but I'll take what I can get." I had a vague feeling that such an idea made no sense, but it only bothered me more when I realized it made no sense to be standing outside my burial crypt as well.

Maybe, I concluded, what made sense in the world of the dead did not always translate into the world of the living.

But I have very little patience to explain anything. I want most of all to speak of what I saw. And when I think of doing so, I immediately think of this dead guy who went by the name of Dodd. I don't remember his first name. But Dodd sticks in my mind like a migraine.

"Let me ask you something," he said to me straight off. They were the first words out of his mouth. He just walked up to me and started up a conversation that I soon learned he had with everyone. "Think about putting a gun to your head. A big one. You pull the trigger, right? BAM! You're dead, right? Isn't that what you'd expect?"

I tried to think through his question. I was sure he was driving at something.

"Well? Am I right?"

"Sure. Bam—you're dead." My delivery of this response was greatly lacking in passion.

"That's what I thought!" He supplied the passion to our conversation. "Jeeze Louise! No one ever said it would hurt! I mean, you pull the trigger, it should all be over."

"It hurt?" I found myself mildly interested in his scenario.

"Hell yes, it hurt! You ain't never felt hurt like that. I screamed and screamed. God, I must have screamed for an hour. And the whole time I was thinking *no one said this would hurt!*"

I watched him shake at the memory. He drew deep breaths in his open mouth and forced the air out through his nose. He was obviously more enraged at not having known how painful his death would be than at the pain itself.

"Don't mind him, that's only Dodd." A thin little man stepped up beside me and waved dismissively as Dodd continued to describe his pain. "He goes on like this forever. Only the new guys listen to him. Everyone else gets tired of hearing it."

"I'm Jack," I said to him, offering my hand.

"Nice to meet you, Jack. I'm Joseph. Sorry, I don't—" he held up a hand and waved away my attempted handshake. To Dodd, he added "Yeah, yeah—hurt like hell. We know. You put a bullet in your brain, you idiot. You thought it would tickle?"

Without touching me, he reached out and guided me away from Dodd. Dodd didn't seem to mind. He just kept on saying over and over "hurt like *Hell!* God!"

We walked down the rows of crypts, moving aside from time to time to allow others to pass. I don't remember when I accepted that there were so many of us walking about in the early darkness of the evening. I knew what we were. No one had to say it aloud. In fact, that was a distinct point to be made. No one did say it aloud. No one dared to mention just what we were. At least that's what I assumed. I came to realize later that most of them simply did not care to say it aloud, as if the whole matter were trivial. There was no spell that might be broken if our true nature were spoken of. But from my own point of view, I felt certain it would be in bad form to say anything.

Joseph led me on past crumbling tombs and one or two weary, cast-iron fences. I had no idea where we were going though I repeatedly asked him that very question. He would never give an answer.

The blue and purplish twilight mixed with the glow of white plaster and marble, highlighting our shapes with an otherworldly aura. This radiance was unnerving to me at first, for it gave off no light beyond the outlines of our bodies. It merely burned within the boundaries of our frames. The total effect gave us the appearance of being lit from within by shrouded firelight. This became more and more apparent as the night grew darker.

We crossed from one crowded lane of crypts to a more spacious avenue. Large crypts with detailed stonework stood like the stately homes in the surrounding Garden District. Beyond these, we came upon a group of low, flat coping tombs. There were a great number of the dead congregating here, the coping tombs being used as benches.

I had imagined Joseph was leading me here to introduce me to someone who might explain what was going on, or at the very least he would tell me this was the best place to spend the night for safety's sake. I wasn't really sure what would be said, but I expected something—anything. I never suspected he would lead me there and then promptly ignore me. Once there, he spoke to one or two of the others then idly wandered away.

I stood at the head of one of the makeshift benches and watched a woman who sat on the far end of it. She sat motionless, staring straight ahead. I turned my head to my right to see just what held her attention. Across the wide avenue sat a tall, narrow crypt with six squares. The whole mausoleum was done in marble. It was expensive work, this was no brick memorial overlaid with plaster. A fat, milky cross sat imposingly on a thin shelf just below the name plates. An inscription in the gable of the roof read *Society for the Relief of Destitute Orphan Boys* with the year 1894 in its center. There was something both noble and heartbreaking at the thought of someone or some group spending so much money and effort on children who had spent their lives here on earth wanting and alone.

"Have you ever spoken to any of them?" I asked her. "The children, I mean."

She turned and gave me a startled and curious look. I saw right away how drawn and tired she looked. Her hair was black, as was her dress. A shadow lay across her and I could not see her hands. After staring at me for an uncomfortable silence she answered me with a shake of her head. I felt as if I'd asked an obviously stupid question.

"They don't come out?" Even as I asked, I knew the answer. I wished I knew why the orphans never came out, but I did not wish to ask a second stupid question.

"I knew one of them," she said softly.

"There are no names on the plates. How do you know?" I thought I had better stop asking questions. I sensed my questions were not only stupid but that they were becoming increasingly insensitive as well.

"He was my child. My little boy." She said nothing more. She had no need to say more. She hadn't been staring at the crypt. She had been weeping before it, quite possibly each and every night for God knew how many years, only she had no more tears. Her tears had run out a very long time ago. Her sobs had ceased to shake her frame as well. All she appeared to have left was the pain and despair that clouded her soul. I wished I had never spoken to her. And yet I wished to know everything; why had the boy been orphaned? Why had he died young? Unable to make such wishes come true, I did the one thing I could do and turned away from her.

"Something the matter?" A tall man stood beside me furiously cleaning his eyeglasses on his shirttail. He held them up to the blackness of the night as if he were looking for spots on them. He glanced down to take his measure of me before returning to the task of making his glasses spotless.

"No. Nothing's wrong. I wouldn't have thought you'd need glasses… anymore." I blurted that last bit out before I remembered how taboo the subject of death seemed to be. I had not meant to make such an obvious allusion to the man's condition. I flushed at my error, but he never seemed to notice it.

"If it's the girl that's bothering you, don't worry over her too much. That's just Marie. She's batty." He felt for a less soiled corner of his shirttail and smothered a lens with it.

"I can understand that," I said with what I hoped would sound like sage understanding, "I'm sure a mother handles the loss of a child with less pragmatism than do fathers."

"You're not seeing things clearly," he said after sliding the glasses on and wrapping them around his ears. "It appears to me you're being made a fool of. It is as clear to me as my own hand in front of my face—Marie's no mother. Never had a son."

"How do you know that?"

"Oh, damn it all." He pulled his glasses off and stuffed them back into the shirttail, vigorously rubbing at the lenses.

I turned away from him as eagerly as I had from the grieving mother. His fanatic craving for spotless lenses baffled me. I hurried away. I must have rudely pushed people out of the way. With a certain detachment, I could hear people complaining as I jostled my way through them. Whether I murmured my apologies to them or not I cannot say. But I continued to push on with a total lack of decorum for maybe two or three minutes.

I eventually regained my composure and walked alone for maybe half an hour. Honestly, time for us dead did not move in the same way it did when our hearts pulsed with blood. I had not been buried with a watch, and so I had no way to prove this. But I had no illusions about how we moved through time. I could see already that the night would drag on far longer than it would have when we were alive. I didn't like that thought. I wanted to get on with it. I felt like a sleepless man who lay feverishly in bed, only too aware that he had seven more hours alone with his thoughts. But what added a great deal of unease to my mind was the realization that I was trapped not just with my own thoughts, but the thoughts of all those dead surrounding me.

William and Thomas were prime examples of this. I found them both standing in the middle of a lane, staring at two crypts that stood so close only weeds fit between them.

William was a large and imposing figure. He stood shaking his head at an ornate cathedral-shaped memorial made of red granite. It was topped with four spires at each of its corners. A high-pitched roof bridged the gap between the spires. Colonnades on both sides of the intricately carved door were covered in stone ivy and flowering vines. William gestured at the ornate structure without turning an eye in my own direction.

"Have you any idea how much that cost? Red Granite, for God's sake. Look at it. I made no provisions for that. She must have mortgaged the house to have that erected. What was she thinking? That woman will be the death of me."

"She must have loved you a great deal." I couldn't keep my mouth shut. But I caught myself in time to say nothing more.

"Loved me? *I've* got nothing to do with it. This is her way of putting on a show for her friends. She'll play it up all the way. They'll be shaking their heads in wonder and admiration at her sacrificial gesture. More'n likely they'll take up a collection for her. Oh, just look at the flower vases. Four of them! Paid full price on all of them, I'd bet."

"I'd take red granite," Thomas said, managing to sound forlorn without serving it up too thick. "Red granite lasts such a long time. Can you believe I've only got brick with plaster smeared all over it. They didn't even bother to add the fake lines that make it look like stone. And why should they have? The plaster's already cracking and flaking off in places. See there? Just under the south eave."

I couldn't see it from where I stood, but I said nothing in reply. I was getting better at that.

"I won't even mention the stele. Unbelievable." He shook his head. I could hear both anger and shame in his words. I thought he did have a valid point about the nameplate. It was sitting on the ground in two pieces. The largest piece leaned against the crypt opening. Behind this, I could see the unevenly placed bricks which had been thrown together in a truly shoddy fashion. Two bricks were missing at the top. The smaller piece of the stele lay flat in the grass.

"Worked nearly every day for forty-three years." William was still talking about money. "Saved everything

I could. The wife spends it on this. Do you see what I mean?"

"No," I answered.

"I refused the doctor's last suggested treatment because I told him I'd be damned before I spent that kind of money. I hadn't spent a lifetime saving money in order to waste it all keeping myself alive. And look. I can tell you, I've researched this. I knew what kind of costs were involved in something this grand. And I know to the penny just how much I had put away. She spent it all. It's all right here."

"Don't let him get to ya," Thomas warned me with a hand on my shoulder. "His loved ones obviously cared enough to put thought and effort into this. It's magnificent. How they must have loved him. My people, on the other hand…" he held his hands out in the direction of his dilapidated vault and nearly growled at what stood before him.

I opened my mouth to ask if his people had the money to spend on his grave but closed it before the words came out. I didn't really want to hear his answer. I could only imagine that no matter their financial situation, he would find some way to demean the choices they had made.

I left them arguing over their troubles and found my way back onto the wide avenue where I'd started earlier that evening. I saw Joseph again. He was leading a short, fat man towards the coping tombs.

"You look like you could use a friend."

I turned towards a very young man who smiled with excitement brimming in his eyes. Despite his near manic enthusiasm, he had a pleasant face.

"Don't get me wrong, but maybe a few answers might satisfy me more than just finding a friend." I was sure I had just said something offensive.

"Don't I know it? Your first night, am I right?" If I'd offended him, he never showed it.

"Yes."

"My first night was worse. I wandered around all night. Had no idea what was going on. I just wanted it to end as soon as possible."

"That's about the sum of my first night," I empathized.

"On, I know what you mean. But mine went beyond that. People came up to me out of nowhere and just whined and complained as if my only purpose were to listen to them cry. I wanted to be their friend, not their counselor."

I saw Joseph heading towards me and I raised my head in recognition. He waved a hand towards my excited companion and shook his head.

"Don't mind him, that's only Carter. He goes on like this forever. No matter what you say, he'll not only know what you mean, but he'll have been through something even bigger than you." To Carter he added, "Nobody cares, man. Nobody cares what you know; nobody cares what you've done. No one wants a friend like that."

Before I knew it, Joseph was gently guiding me back towards the now crowded set of benches. It occurred to me he probably had no idea why he was leading me there. But I didn't resist him. I wanted to find Marie. I had decided the eyeglass-cleaning specter had not known what he was talking about.

"I'm sorry about your son," I said softly as I sat down beside her. She didn't say anything in response, and I gladly remained silent as well. I stared at the blank nameplates of the destitute orphan boys and waited with her.

Behind us, a man complained to no one in particular that he was there by mistake. Some trivial technical error had been made in some vague, far-off place and here he was stuck amongst the dead. I tried to block out his voice and just concentrate on Marie and her son. I couldn't have said why. Maybe because she was the only one not saying anything. Everyone else had something to say. Even Joseph seemed hell-bent on pointing out who should be ignored. I too had felt the urge to be always speaking, even if it had always been to ask a question.

But not Marie. The few words she had spoken had only been in reply to my own questions. Maybe she had run out of words when she had run out of tears. I didn't know for certain. And I didn't have to.

My thoughts turned towards her son and the other orphaned boys. Why did they never come out? Surely they had something to say? They, more than any of us, had reason to complain: alone, a life of want. Had they ever learned to accept it? Maybe in fact they had. Surrounded by so many who wanted so much, I began to suspect just what set these orphans apart. They did not demand fairness; they had learned long ago how fickle life could be. They did not crave the finer things in life; the basics were hard enough to hold onto. All I had heard and seen that night had been the empty shells of men seeking and desiring what they could not have; before or after death. One desired to control money he no longer held. Another had wanted to make and impress a friend. A mother wanted her son. And even I had wanted something strong enough to pull me from my grave. I wanted to understand. I wanted to know why.

But there before us lay a tiny group of boys who wanted nothing in death, as they had learned to do in life.

I only became aware of the tear that rolled down my cheek when Marie reached up and wiped it gently onto her hand. She rubbed at it with her thumb, rolling it around until it was gone.

She still had no words to say. But for that moment, she had taken the tear and it had been enough. It was something I knew for certain, though I would never understand. And I hoped that I too could find it to be enough.

Resurrection

I'd been very disappointed to discover that Commander's Palace was still closed for repairs a full year after Hurricane Katrina had assaulted New Orleans. It was my first chance after the storm to return to the city of my youth, and I had been assured by old friends that Commander's would be open for business. After standing on Washington Avenue, staring at the cacophony of workmen and construction traffic for five or six minutes, I reluctantly faced the fact that I would not be dining on turtle soup at one of New Orleans's most venerable restaurants for lunch.

The image of that grand old man being brought back from its storm-ravaged condition ruined what appetite I'd had. With little interest in finding other dining arrangements, I turned around and my gaze fell upon the iron gates of Lafayette Cemetery Number One.

At least, it seemed, the old bone yard was still intact. I decided I would step inside the gates and get a little exercise. Most importantly, I wanted to cast off the somber spirit I'd felt touring the still broken streets of my city. And the Cities of the Dead could do just that. Strange as it may sound, I had always found a walk through those quiet fields of monuments to be an uplifting experience.

And this was why I had been walking the grassy lanes among the ancient tombs of New Orleans. And that was where I met the old man.

He'd been standing just inside the Prytania Street gates. He was dressed in a wool suit, a bit heavy for the still warm September days, I thought. His hair was neatly trimmed, his face closely shaved. In a word, he looked normal. He gave every indication of being in his right mind. He'd been standing perfectly still.

I had not noticed him right away and likely would have missed him had he not spoken to me.

"Young man," he said in a clear voice, with that familiar tone that let me know he called everyone *young man*, "I'd like to have a word with you, if you have the time."

I said something obscure, trying not to commit to anything. I liked his face. I had always been drawn to older people. I'd always wanted to know what had etched such deep lines upon their lives; what hidden strengths and desires lay dormant under time's mask of old age. I should have readily accepted his intrusion had I not been so keen on a lighthearted walk under that September sun.

"Still hot," he closed one eye and tried to look directly into the sun. "I like that. I can't get enough of it—the warmth of the sun."

"I can do without it at times," I said as I read the inscription of the crypt in front of us. Magnolia trees shifted their weight above us in the light breeze as if bored with our conversation. I stepped into their shade as the old man took a deliberate step away from it. He looked as if he feared the cool of the shade.

"I'll take the sun. The heat." He sucked in the warm air, as if his whole body were absorbing the heat.

I tried to amble away from him, showing great interest in the crumbling graves. I did not think he had followed me, but as I passed a plot full of high grass and a rusted fence leaning on its perimeter, he spoke to me again. He was only a step away from me.

"You've walked straight to it." He extended one hand and pointed to the grave. "I really think you ought to stay for a little while. I could tell you about this one.

The tour guides will tell you no one knows anything about these abandoned plots. While other crypts are cared for by the families, it's generally believed there had once been a crypt of some kind here but time and neglect have allowed it to fall to pieces. And now, they say, even the pieces are gone. Nothing left but weeds and grass, maybe a foundation of stone under all that growth. The fence here," the old man lowered his hand to stroke the black iron but stopped short of actually touching it, "once strong and erect with diligent purpose, now only a broken sentinel that has forgotten what it had ever been guarding."

"I remember hearing something like that."

"Guesswork. Very poor guesswork. I could tell you the truth. I'm getting too old. And someone needs to know the truth."

I looked at the sad empty plot. Surrounded by crypts four and five feet high, the little patch of overgrown grave looked like the remains of a forgotten garden. A few bright green fingers of vines had found their way up onto the fence. A few purple blooms were still hanging on. The overall effect was not a garden of life but a waste of decay. Even the insects that flew over it chose to fly on in search of something better. As if to prove the point, the one lone dragonfly that had landed on that plot was now hanging upside down in an ancient spider web, a dry and brittle testimony for all to see.

"Someone should clear this off. It wouldn't take much effort."

"Yes," the old man nodded as if he approved of my remark, "and yet no one does it. They have begun to repair so many crypts. Delicate, difficult work. But here—"

"A gas trimmer would do it." I kicked at the freshly cut lane beneath us. "Someone's cutting the grass. Are they not allowed to cut it? Does the family ask that it be left like that?"

"There's no family. No stipulations upon the grave." He raised an eyebrow at me.

"But you know why?"

"I did not say that. I only said I know the truth."

He had me. I could see no way around it by then. My curiosity had been tickled enough that I could not have walked away. I held out my hand and told him my name.

"I'm Kenneth Linaker. I once lived here," he said, taking my hand.

"I did too, a long time ago. But I haven't lived in New Orleans for many years."

"You misunderstand me," his eyes caught mine, and I could not look away, "I once lived here." He waved a hand at the tombs that surrounded us.

"I'm going back a long ways, now." He began to speak as if he stood before a grand audience. In fact, it seemed as if he were addressing the whitewashed tombs instead of me. "Forty, fifty years ago. A very long time. But then, I don't guess that matters much to a place like this. Fifty years is a summer's day, I suppose. But not to me. I've made each day of each year as long as a summer's day.

"But not back then. I never did. I worked. Played. All of it without giving a thought to my life. Everything just came to me. A wife. Children. A career. It all came as easy to me as the ruin that followed. And with as little effort, I ended here, amongst the dead."

I suppose my facial expression gave away my disbelief. He redirected his words to me.

"I'm not out of my mind. I never said I'd been dead. I only said I ended here. I was destitute and sleeping here at night. I'd made this my home. Perhaps I had known from the start how badly I wanted to die.

"I won't bore you with the details of my misery. How my wife and children died, it makes little difference.

Is there a way your heart can die that would make it any more bearable? Don't ask 'did they suffer?' Or 'did those responsible pay?' If you've ever lost the ones you love the dearest, you'd know it makes no difference! My family was dead. That's what is most important.

"That would have been enough, but there had to be more. The news of my financial ruin came as no shock. By that time, I had come to believe that nothing good in life would survive. And I was being proved right. The only real shock was waking every morning and discovering that I was still alive. That I was not going to be let off easy with a quick death. No fatal disease overcame me. No absurd accident ended my life. It was evident I was meant to live out my misery for a very long time.

"And so, at the deepest part of my fall, I came here. Alone. I lived as if I were dead. I slept there on that step where you sit. And anywhere else I came to rest. I don't remember always how or what I ate. There were those who took pity on me. I made no effort to solicit charity, but then I never turned it down either.

"I had lost all track of time. I was not aware of how long I'd been in that state. But occasionally, others would join me. I was never eager to share my home with them, no matter that it was a graveyard. I could see too

23

much life in them. No one shared my nearness to death. At least not until Burt.

"Burt was different. I sensed that immediately. I will not say he had an air of death about him. No, that would be too dramatic—too expected. But there was an absence of life about him. I'm not talking about physical things." Here he stopped his narrative in order to bark sharply at me. "Don't do that!"

I had placed a hand on the leaning gate of the abandoned plot. His reproof was harsh enough to make me jerk back my hand. In doing so I scraped the heel of my right hand on a rough patch of rusted black iron. I wanted to scold him for startling me, but one look in his eyes told me I had better just keep my mouth shut.

"No," he continued on as if he had not just disciplined me like a misbehaving schoolboy, "I'm not talking about physical things. He moved, he spoke, he might have even laughed a time or two. But in everything he did, Burt did it without an inner light. There was a void surrounding him. His words fell from his mouth without power. He could laugh or cry out in a stiff wind and neither the laugh nor the cry would be carried any distance. He had no past. That was common for many of us then. He existed without a future—that was not so rare. But I tell you the truth when I say he had no *present*. He had never been, he never would be, and he was not *at that moment*. Burt did not exist.

"And that is the very reason I stayed with him. I was tired of the whiners, babbling *ad nauseam* about their pitiful lives. I understood their misery. I was, in fact, living with the same regrets and broken heart. But I had no desire to sit mired in the filth of my ruined life. Oh, I had no desire to pick myself up and trudge gloriously ahead into a shining new day. A rebuilt future seemed much more likely to fall down around me than the solid life I had built on the first go-around. And so I liked Burt immensely. I simply had to discover his secret about how to live outside of the present without hiding in the past or hoping for a future. That was the key for which I was willing to wait.

"I watched him. I listened to him. Spent days and weeks with him, just sitting with him and observing everything about him. His relationship to food unnerved me at first. Where many of us look forward to our next meal, talk about it with anticipation, Burt never gave his next meal a single thought. When I presented him with some bit of candy or sweet snack, he never expressed satisfaction or delight. He simply accepted the item and placed it in his mouth. He never commented on the taste, never nodded with appreciation. Neither did he show discontent or distaste. Eating was simply something that happened which demanded no comment. It was all very baffling to me. I was always snacking on one thing or another growing up. It was never long after we ate a meal that I was already asking my mother what we would be eating at the next meal. I could never take a bite without commenting on the taste, or how fresh or stale it was. Even after I married, I was forever speaking about the most routine of refreshments. My wife made coffee in the exact same manner every day of our marriage. And yet watching Burt made me realize I never drank a cup of my wife's coffee without saying 'oh, that's good coffee.' As if the world were waiting for my running commentary on everything I ate or drank.

"Burt accepted everything around him in the same way. If we were sitting in the rain, I could never detect him acknowledging it in any fashion. The heaviest downpour could crash down upon us out of a clear night sky, and then cease as abruptly—Burt never said a word. Never cast one annoyed glance toward heaven.

"He was affected by nothing. And I wanted it! Whatever he had, I wanted it! I, Kenneth Linaker was tired of life—all of its pain and disappointment, its dreadfully repetitive routine. The pointlessness of a rising and setting sun. Burt had seen as much hurt and loss as I. I had been able to glean that much from him. But he was never bound by it. He did not run from it. He never appeared ready to end his life in abject defeat. He was simply immune to life's bite.

"And in time, I began to feel it. I began to take a step into Burt's empty realm. One by one the cares of life and the passions of my soul fell from me as leaves from a tree. But even as I withdrew from the world around me I could still see that Burt withdrew even further. He ceased to speak. It became difficult to get him to eat. As I found peace in my newfound void, I watched Burt grow more and more detached."

Linaker stopped speaking and stared intensely at the abandoned plot and its overgrown weeds.

"Is this where he was buried?" I asked hastily.

"I'll tell you. There are waking moments when dreams invade reality. And desperate dreams that reality mercifully interrupts. The former may confuse us for a heartbeat—the latter diffuses the fantastic almost instantaneously. But both are easily distinguishable once they have occurred. The chimera is gone with a shake of the head. We know we have but dreamed.

"What I tell you now was no dream. Although it should only have been just that, a dream. I was sleeping. I don't deny it. Just over there, a few crypts from here, I was lying on the grass. It was a warm night. Right there. Burt was here, sleeping just a few steps from this plot of ground." Linaker's throat sounded dry. He licked his upper lip before continuing.

"I became aware, still asleep, of heat. A great powerful heat. I felt it all over, suffocating, overwhelming. The dry and tangled growth over the abandoned grave shriveled in the heat then bent and collapsed upon itself. It popped and crackled like the crushing of dry bones. And from the center of it, a smoldering glow appeared. The old weeds and grass seethed—as if they were angry and alive. This menace burst into flames and I sat up. I was wide-awake. As the flames grew in size, the plot under this blaze split open with a tearing and rending that bespoke of a great and unearthly pressure. The force of this smashed open the wrought iron gates, which gaped wide in mocking welcome. I watched the earth that had been pushed aside at the creation of the small chasm begin to slide into it. The heat was great enough to make me believe that the edge of the chasm was melting into it.

"All of this had occurred in just a few seconds. It took me longer than that to realize Burt was too close to the wide-open gates. The heat prevented me from leaping to his aid. He lay perfectly still. He was just as stoic as ever. His eyes stayed open in half-slits as the lip of the chasm continued to pour slowly over the edge. It dragged easily at Burt, who did not even watch as he was dragged closer and closer to that burning maw.

"And then, from within the flames, a figure arose. I will not describe him. I refuse to. But I will say he was big enough that he almost filled the hole that by then had grown to the size of nearly the entire plot. Cloaked in smoke, this figure rose over the immobile form of Burt. A hand slid out from under the shifting cloak and lightly touched Burt's head. Burt shrieked as if his head had been doused in flames. I did not shout in alarm. I watched, amazed that Burt had actually reacted to the touch. For the briefest of moments, I felt pride that I could watch such a scene with some of Burt's detachment.

"That dark master of the chasm closed his fingers over Burt's throat and pulled him through the open gates. I could no longer watch calmly. Burt's shrieking had transformed into a wail of primal, feral terror. He was being dragged on his back. His feet already at the lip of the fissure. The feet kicked spasmodically as if they might be able to douse the fiery pit through sheer desperation. Burt clawed viciously at the hand that held him. He jerked his head from side to side, eyes twisting to both sides, straining for any sign of salvation. Once, he twisted enough to catch a glimpse of me. I held my breath, afraid to hear him call out to me; scream my name. He didn't. He couldn't. He was already on fire by then. The noise that erupted from him was matched only by the discordant and pitiful screams flowing from the pit.

"I tried to help him. The heat literally pushed me away at every attempt I made to reach him. His black enshrouded executioner ignored his frantic fits and did not stop until he had completely dragged Burt into that burning gate of Hell. I fell to my knees, staring at the rapidly disfiguring form that had been my companion.

"The Black Lord, (for who else could it have been?), grinning at his prey, turned to look at me. The grin turned to cold emotionless stone. Despite the heat surrounding us, I felt a chill run through me. 'I will come back for you. Fear not!' He laughed at his own mockery and descended into the melting pool of smoke and terror."

I waited for Linaker to say more. "And did he?" I prompted him.

"Did he what?"

"Come back?" Even as I asked it I realized how foolish that question sounded.

"I have no idea. Did you think I stuck around to see if he would?" Linaker turned his face to the warmth of the sun and inhaled deeply. "A day hasn't passed that I haven't tried to embrace every bit of life I could. I have learned from my past. I embrace my present. And I hope for my future. Will I die? Of course. But for now, I am alive. So very alive!"

The Imposter

Thomas lay on his back. He could smell rain, or at least things made wet by the rain: wet moss, wet iron, and even wet stone. He turned his head; found there was no room to turn it completely. His face brushed against soft fabric. It might have been silk. Whatever it was, it wasn't wet. The wet came from outside. The odor was faint yet distinct.

He did not lie in the dark for long, wondering where he was or what had happened. He knew where he was. He had made the arrangements himself. It was impossible to mistake his surroundings. He was in his family's crypt. Though it was impossible to tell, he knew he was on the top tier of the burial chamber. He even knew who was directly below him: his father. And below his father was his nephew, the young boy he had never had the chance to meet. There were too many others to name who were now just dust, heaped together in the family crypt's shallow *caveau*.

The silk that surrounded him was dark blue. Thomas could not see it, but he knew what it was. He had chosen the dark blue because the light blue had looked too old, like something from the nineteen-fifties. He had decided it was too tacky, too worn. It would have made the casket appear as if it had been left out in the sun.

They were all gone, he thought, hearing nothing beyond the brick and plaster walls. Was it very late? If they had followed his schedule they would have held the service at ten, and he would have been sealed within the crypt before noon. Had anyone lingered? Had they all hurried back to their personal business without a backwards glance?

Conscious of his surroundings, he wondered why he was only now aware of his present state. Why not before the service? Maybe during it? He would have liked to hear what had been said. To see who had come and who had not. Why was he only now waking up?

He could not stand to lie there any longer. He wanted to know so many things. At least he might get an idea how things had gone by the number of flowers arrayed around the steps. There might be cards to read.

Thomas left the crypt, a maneuver far more difficult than he had expected, and gazed around at the grey light of a cloudy afternoon. No rain fell, but it had been falling only a few minutes before. A few drops of rain still clung to the votive shelf beside the nameplate. Every so often one of them finally let go and dropped to the steps.

The steps were empty. There were no flowers.

"How long have I been in there?" He felt cold inside. It was conceivable he had been lying there for days, or even years. There was no reason he couldn't have been lying in that crypt for one hundred years.

There was evidence to contradict this theory. Lying just off to the left of the crypt was a small plastic guitar. It was no longer than Thomas's thumb; a gumball-machine toy. The miniature black guitar lay fret down in the grass. Thomas picked it up and brushed off mud that marred its surface. He stood it up on the top step, leaning it against the crypt face.

He had always left the little guitars in that manner. This one he had left only a few weeks ago. Thomas knew it could not be later than October. He had left the guitar on the top step on September the 10th, the anniversary of his father's death. The guitar showed no sign of having been in the weather for an extended period of time. And most years they did not last longer than four weeks. Within four weeks, someone was sure to steal the little guitar. He didn't care. It had given him a reason to come back with one every year.

But if it had not been more than four or five weeks, then where were the flowers from his service? Most flowers were not stolen, certainly not within the first four weeks. And Thomas could clearly remember two weeks after the anniversary of his father's death, which meant he could have only been dead a few weeks at the very most.

No flowers? Was it possible no one had sent flowers? It wasn't that flowers meant so much to him, but the absence of them was palpable. Why would no one send him flowers?

He nervously struck out from the crypt, heading in the direction of the east gate. Silence reigned over the houses of the dead. It was still afternoon and Thomas had a feeling that no one would be out until after dark.

The rain had obviously chased away the living. Thomas was alone, and he felt it far more than he would have liked.

He stopped at the open double gates. He couldn't leave, of course. He understood that. But hoped for some sign of what was happening. Something that could tell him what had happened.

After watching for a space of time that he could not measure (he wondered if time had lost all meaning for him now) he gave up and returned to his crypt. He had discovered nothing.

Thomas was on his back again, only this time he had heard a voice. Faint, muffled, but a voice all the same. And just as the odors of wet moss and wet stone had been faint but distinct, so too had this voice been faint but distinct. It could not have been anything else. He had heard *her* voice. Nancy had called his name.

Thomas lay perfectly still, with no need to hold his breath in order to hear more clearly. She called to him again, though she sounded further away than she had at first.

"Thomas, wait."

Had his heart still beat it would have hammered in his chest. Did she know he could hear her? Would she be able to see him?

Getting out of the crypt was just as difficult as the first time. This frustrated him, and he worried she would be gone before he could slip free from the whitewashed brick. She was leaving, and he would miss her.

Once free, he stumbled into the grass lane, looking first east, then back to the west. He did not see her, but she could not have gone very far. She would have come in through the east gate. He ran between the rows of crypts, frantic to see her, filled with terror at the prospect of missing her.

She was already at the gate by the time he came within sight of it. She was leaving, hand in hand with a man. Thomas felt ice on his brow despite the late morning sun and his short sprint. When she let go of the man's hand he reached up and pulled her close against him. They turned and headed towards the foot of Canal Street.

Thomas tried to hurry, tried to get to the gate in time to see who was with her. The man was familiar, though only vaguely. Once at the gate, he tried to lean forward in order to see around the burial wall. He could not see them, though he could hear her purr after the man muttered a few words.

Thomas wandered down a grassy lane, then back up another. He paid no attention to where he was going. He was too intent on trying to remember just what he had seen.

The man was about her height, but broader at the shoulders. He had sandy brown hair that hung down to his shoulders. That was disturbing to Thomas. That was the way Thomas had worn his hair since high school. A simple thought waited in the back of Thomas's mind, ready to be called upon when Thomas was ready for the simple truth. But Thomas explored alternate possibilities, refusing to acknowledge the existence of the simple explanation.

With whom would she have been? Thomas had no male relatives in the city. Neither did Nancy. A friend? Co-worker? He had seen that man's coat before. The more he thought about it, the more he realized he had more than just seen such a coat before. He had worn one just like it.

Thomas stopped walking, beside a low coping tomb with an open-faced stone book perched on its front edge. He read the inscription. *A Faithful Husband and Friend.*

No, Nancy would not be seeing someone so soon after his death. And she was never one to purr around anyone but Thomas. *A Comfortable Husband and Friend.* Had Nancy added anything to his nameplate? He had not paid the slightest attention to it.

Overcome with weariness—it seemed the dead were not meant to be moving around for long periods of time—Thomas returned to his crypt. He was shocked to see nothing on the faceplate after his father's date of death. What was taking so long? His name should have been added by then. Nancy was being taken advantage of. If Thomas were still alive, he would not have allowed that to happen.

Before forcing his way back inside, he noted the little guitar was gone.

He made many more attempts to see Nancy, though most voices he heard turned out to be tourists or caretakers. But each time he scrambled out of the tomb, he did so with less effort. He was getting better at bending the material world to accommodate his otherworldly needs.

He knew All Saints Day was coming soon. Nancy would come. They had both been loyal caretakers of the family crypt, and though he was now dead, she was sure to make an appearance. And why not? Especially now that he lay inside. She would not miss his first year on the other side.

Thomas needed to rest. He needed to be able to leave the crypt and watch for her. He could not hope to catch her after she arrived. That would require a massive effort. He lay in the dark, surrounded by brick and mortar, and willed himself to rest. It was not easy. A great racket arose from the neighboring crypts all night long. Thomas refused to take a peek at the antics of Hallow's Eve.

He was ready early. She would come early, she always had. Thomas wanted to wait for her at the gate, but the effort would have restricted his available time outside the vault. Instead, he sat down on the crypt's single step and waited.

He had nearly drifted off to sleep when he heard her voice. She was coming. Thomas rose, his fingers fidgeting with themselves.

She took his breath away as she came around a corner, no matter that he no longer had breath. He held out a shaking hand, hoping against reason that she might feel a whisper of his touch.

Before he could touch her, the man came around the corner behind her. Thomas's hand dropped in shock as he recognized her companion. In that same instant, Nancy spoke.

"Oh, Thomas, the guitar is gone again."

"Maybe my father takes them," her companion suggested, laughing at his own idea. "Oh, look. Some of the plaster has cracked on this corner. That's new."

Thomas couldn't help but look down at the cracked corner. Was that a result of his early efforts to escape the crypt? He had been clumsy those first few times.

"Looks as if someone ran into it." Nancy bent down, examining the damage. "Do you know how to mend something like this?"

"No, but I guess I could try."

Thomas forced himself to stop staring at the cracked plaster and stared hard at the young man standing beside Nancy. Had she called him Thomas?

"I wonder if Ron and Carol will come by today." Her companion put out his hand and ran it along the stele, over the name of the nephew.

"Carol said they might, but later. Will your dad like these new flowers I bought? I thought I'd try them." She set a bouquet of orange flowers into a stone vase at the corner of the crypt.

"Sure, I guess." The man wasn't looking at the flowers. Instead, he had knelt down and begun pulling at a few stray bits of grass growing between the stones on the walkway.

"Do you like them?" she asked.

"When I die, don't put flowers out here for me. I want a Muffuletta from Central Grocery. And don't wait until All Saints Day. Bring me one every month." He smiled at her with a crooked grin. "You suppose they allow conjugal visits?"

"That's crass," she smacked his shoulder. "Don't talk like that here. Your father might hear you."

"And my grandmother, and my grandfather, and—" the man reached out a finger and looked over the list on the faceplate—"Horace Walpool, whoever he is."

Thomas stood beside them, unable to fathom what he was seeing. What did this mean? Who was this man with Nancy? The better question was: *why was Thomas in the crypt?* Had he really died?

He wanted to take Nancy in his arms. She would feel him. She had to. She had to realize that the man she was with was not her husband. Maybe Thomas could stop this man. But how? What could he do? Whatever it was, it would have to be soon. They were nearly finished cleaning up the gravesite. Nancy never liked lingering around the crypt.

"Come here," the man said softly, reaching out and pulling her to him. His arms wrapped around her and she leaned against him. "I like the new flowers. And yeah, dad will love them."

"You're just saying this to make up for your visiting comment."

"I'm saying that because I needed a reason to put my arms around you." He leaned forward, kissing her forehead.

Thomas stared at the two lovers in desperation, unable to think of what he could do. He could feel himself tiring, and knew he had no time to work out the best solution. Whatever he did, it would have to be soon.

"Let's get out of here, huh?" He kissed her again, this time on her neck. She purred.

Thomas looked away, focusing on the cracked corner of the crypt. He had an idea, but there was no way to tell if it would work. The only thing he could do was try. He did not hesitate. He had to work as quickly as possible.

Rushing forward, he surged between Nancy and his imposter. Wrapping his arms around the man, Thomas focused his will on the cracked plaster. It would not have to crack more, the gap was big enough. It would just take a readjustment. He backed through the narrow opening, his arms still fiercely clutching at his doppelganger, his feet ramming into the stone steps, propelling him backwards. He felt the man's form begin to buckle, to collapse and twist within the tapered breach in the plaster.

Thomas could hear Nancy scream his name. But which Thomas was she calling? He could not stop to think about it. His energy was draining rapidly. He would have to get inside the crypt as soon as inhumanly possible.

The double, Thomas refused to call him by name, had not gone without a fight. He was struggling, kicking and biting wildly at Thomas. But with his arms pinned at his side, he could not stop Thomas from burrowing deeper into the crypt.

Nancy's voice was far away now. Thomas could hear her calling, but her words were unclear.

Hidden in the silk-lined coffin, Thomas could no longer see. His enemy was still with him; Thomas's arms still locked around him. The space was too cramped for him to let go. Even if it were possible, he would never let go. Not for a very long time.

The Unbroken Seal

(*Danse Macabre 62, Anvil*)

Paul was dead and terribly alone. He had planned it that way despite his family's attempts to change his mind. And even though they had turned out to be right he wasn't about to admit it out loud.

And if he did, no one would hear him.

He had planned it that way.

On the day he had purchased his tomb he had ordered out Chinese for an impromptu celebration. All of his dreams were coming true. He had worked hard, saved his money, and finally left his hometown for the Big Easy. *Naw'lins*. Call it whatever you like, even the dreaded Yankee's *New Or-lee-ands*, for Paul it was home. And he would never have another.

The tomb was just one more step to solidifying his life below sea level. At first he had lived in one of those cracker box apartment complexes out in Metairie, but that was only until he had gotten his feet on the ground. By year two he had moved into Faubourg Marigny, and he fit in like a native.

Without a past to anchor him to the Crescent City, he had decided to make an anchor of his future. He spent two months touring the aboveground cemeteries of New Orleans. There were a surprising number of them, and he wanted to look at each and every one. By the time he had decided to use St. Roch's, he knew he had made the right decision.

His family did not understand. His mother cried. What they did understand was that he would never be coming back to them. Not in life or in death. His father never complained, but Paul knew he had hurt the old man. But he did not let that sway him from his plan. They pleaded with him to reconsider. He had been too young and brash even to consider it. Did they think he was still a child? As a measure of his independence he refused to tell them which cemetery he had chosen. He would build a new family, one that *did* understand him. One that would be worthy to mourn his loss.

The tomb was quite a deal. He had managed to buy a crypt built for a family that had subsequently moved to California. It was larger than he needed, but

Paul decided that once he found a wife and they had children the crypt would be put to good use for many generations to come.

It was an elegant pitched-roof tomb, its brickwork whitewashed recently enough so that the outer shell did not look as if it had just fallen off the truck. An angel knelt atop its truncated façade, wings partially extended, hands grasping a stone bouquet.

On his days off from work, Paul would occasionally visit his tomb, picking the dead leaves out of the surrounding gravel or sweeping away the debris left by a heavy rain. Paul liked to imagine that the inhabitants of St. Roch's gathered outside their crypts at night in order to tell stories from their varied and completed lives. He knew they would accept him as one of their own. There was no reason for them not to. He was, after all, now one of them.

And then on a Wednesday, far sooner than he had expected, Paul took up residence in his tomb. He had been leaving work, or arriving there (he couldn't remember which one it was), when he abruptly lost touch with his surroundings. Time passed; a long, empty time, and then he had awakened in his tomb.

He was unhappy to discover that no one was there to explain to him why he had passed on. He only really became angry when he discovered he could not get out of the crypt. That he was actually in his crypt was a fact that he did not at first grasp. He was forced to work out his situation in the dark; the kind of black dark that city dwellers rarely experienced. But black dark it was, and Paul did not know if his eyes were opened or closed.

He lay on a soft bed of cool fabric, head resting on a pillow of the same material. He was blocked on either side by that same silkiness; it was above him as well. An insane image came to mind; that of an oversized stuffed Alligator—a child's plaything—slowly digesting Paul after having swallowed him whole. Paul refocused on the silky sides of his prison—or was it satin? He had forever been able to mix up the two fabrics.

Though the walls on either side of him held firm, he was relieved to find that the top of his cell relented under focused pressure. Before long, he was able to sit up and grip the sides of what was now, quite obviously, his coffin.

Paul was surprised at how quickly he came to accept the fact of the casket. (Coffin was harder to accept, and the subtle change to *casket* was necessary for his peace of mind.) He felt a certain pride in knowing that he was not going to spend his time whining over his early death. It wouldn't hurt to get a basic explanation, but he wasn't going to obsess over it.

The family crypt was big enough that once the entrance gate was pulled open, a casket could be placed on a dais to the left, and a second could be placed on the right. By slow, careful sweeps of his hands, he could tell he was on the right side—the cold stone wall felt clammy and he wiped his fingers against his pant leg. It must have been winter. Was that the last season he could remember? It didn't seem right, though it was the only explanation for the cold, wet walls.

Paul wanted to lift himself from the casket but he wasn't sure just how far off the floor the casket was raised. A little light would help. He hadn't expected death to be so lightless. If he had known, he wouldn't have had the stained glass window at the back of the crypt blocked in. When he had purchased the crypt, he had not wanted the glass window; he was sure he would be buried with a few valuables and he wanted to keep them secure. The window just begged to be used by thieves. And so the stonemason, who had replaced the old family name out front on the stele with his own, agreed to block up the window to make sure his sanctuary remained inviolate.

In order to keep up his spirit, Paul refused to grow irritated about the window. Instead, he chuckled at his reasoning in life. The worry about valuables had been predicated on the fact that he would have a wife interred beside him, and she would be adorned with the majority of the jewelry.

But there was no wife. None to precede him in death. None to follow after. He had not been quite ready for a helpmeet yet. He was to have chosen one after the house had been finished. Yet the house had never been built. Paul had known where he would build it, had in fact set the wheels in motion to purchase the lot. In eighteen months it would have been completed and ready for him and a wife. There would have been room for children.

But that was all beside the point. He didn't need a wife now, just a bit of light. Without light, he was forced to climb awkwardly out of the casket, nearly knocking it over. The heavy wood held to its perch, however, and Paul was finally able to stand in the center of the crypt. The ceiling, vaulted as it was, was still just inches from Paul's head, which sat atop his six foot one inch frame. He did not need to stoop, but in the darkness, the urge to do so was impossible to ignore. He bent forward and stepped towards the entrance.

He faced an arched door which was split down the middle. Both sides of the door opened with two brass handles. Beyond that was a black iron gate. He knew all of this though he was surrounded by that constant black darkness. The doors were made of a metal alloy, which one he could not recall offhand. All he could remember was that it was both light and strong; the two doors swung easily on their hinges, but a strong storm wouldn't force them open.

Reaching out blindly, he felt for and found the two brass handles. Taking hold of them as if he were a biker grasping the handles of his Harley, he gave them both a strong twist. The brass handles refused to be turned.

Paul let go of them and cocked his head in the dark. They were locked, of course. How could he have forgotten that precaution? The black iron gate was locked as well. All according to Paul's specifications. It had not concerned him when he was alive. A locked door should not have been a problem for a spirit. Yet already, in this first moment of his afterlife, Paul *knew* that he had been wrong. He could not pass blithely through the stones. There would be none of that kind of behavior. There were no explanations needed on this point. That cold clammy feeling from the walls began to seep into the deep cavity of his soulcage. He stepped back from the doors, making sure to stay away from the walls that surrounded him as if he could ward off his rising panic.

Perhaps it was simply a matter of timing. Did the sun still burn in the sky above? Would he find his prison-crypt open once the day was done? The question seemed rhetorical, so simple was the answer. Paul began to feel better immediately. It had been a close thing, being locked up in isolation. Would it have lasted for eternity? God knows he would have gone insane. It would not have taken very long, either. Just knowing he was stranded in that black chamber would have driven him mad. All of his planning would have been his own demise.

Paul erupted into brief laughter. How could he have panicked so quickly? Surely there were spirits in the neighborhood who would have giggled at his immaturity. Thank God he hadn't taken to screaming for help. It would have been a lousy way to meet the folks next door.

For a moment Paul had the funniest feeling that his worry over this near-disaster had gone too far. He thought he really could hear laughter, muffled as it was. And it was definitely not his own. This time he chastened his panic before it could gain an inch on him. The neighbors were not laughing at him. No one was out. The sun must still be in charge of the day. Paul placed his hands upon his casket, intent on climbing back in for some rest.

A knock sounded on the doors. A dull, heavy knock.

Surely the gardeners were not in the habit of knocking on the crypt doors.

"Who is it?" Paul was keenly aware of how absurd his question sounded.

Another knock followed by silence and then a third knock.

Paul approached the entrance and leaned forward until his brow hit the door.

"Hello?" He raised his voice. Turning his head, he pressed an ear against the cold metal. A voice spoke, though it was impossible to understand it.

"Say that again!" Paul shouted.

And whoever stood outside his crypt did just that. The words were faint, but Paul could make them out.

"I don't know. I'm sure there's one in there now. Been there for weeks. You think he can't get out?"

"Prob'ly just a loner. You know the type." This from a second voice.

Paul held still, willing them to speak louder.

"Maybe he hasn't had a visitor yet."

"Yes, it would explain why he hasn't come out. But for pity's sake, he's been here so long. Surely someone came—"

"Well, if they haven't, they will soon, I'm sure. I hope so, for this fella's sake."

Paul hit the door with his fist. It didn't hurt, but it didn't make much noise either. He listened as the two voices moved off to the side of the crypt and around to the back. He followed them, his ear now pressed hard against the new blocks that covered the window.

"I remembered a window here."

"Sure, was one a long time ago, when it was empty."

"Think this fella inside walled it off?"

"Maybe. He might be one of those private sorts, doesn't like company."

Paul pulled away from the blocks and ran his hand over the seams where each block met another. The stonemason had done a decent enough job, and there were no edges that could be exploited.

"We'll find out soon enough. When the seal is broken, and he is allowed to leave his chamber, he'll either come out of his own accord, or he won't."

"I see many of the others are out now." The voice faded even further, as if the speaker were walking away. "Hello, Miss Grivet!"

Paul heard many different voices now, none of them distinguishable.

The dead did meet! They were coming out! But what had the one speaker meant when he spoke of a seal being broken?

"Yes, this one right here." The first speaker was back. "We think he's still bound inside. No visitors, you know."

"A man with a crypt this large obviously has a family," a female voice responded with surprising strength. "He's sure to have a visitor soon, and then he'll be free to come out and introduce himself. Until then, he will have to be patient. That is always a good lesson for new spirits. And it is to our advantage."

"How so?" came the muffled reply.

"If a spirit must wait an uncomfortably long time for his first visitor, it is most always his own fault. These new spirits come to realize what poor bonds of friendship they built in their days of the Sun. Once finally released from their self-imposed confinement, they are far more willing to build bonds of friendship with us, their new neighbors. I've seen it many, many times."

"I'm sure you have, Miss Grivet. You've been in residence here for many more years than I."

"We shall let him stew, as they say." The woman laughed, a light, delicate sound that was vaporous enough to penetrate Paul's dark cell.

"Shall we join the others? "

"Only if you agree to dance with me this evening."

Their voices grew faint as did their laughter.

Paul waited, his ear smashed against his cold prison wall. The woman's voice had carried a great deal of kindness, despite her amusement at Paul's isolation. Surely she would return. She was, perhaps, playing a joke on him. A friendly prank on a new neighbor. She couldn't possibly have been speaking truthfully.

He sank to the floor, though he couldn't have said when. He had no way to mark the passage of time. He could, however, be certain that neither the man nor the woman returned to attempt communication with him.

Hours later, perhaps days later, Paul crawled awkwardly back into his coffin. It was no use trying to call it anything other than that. *Casket* seemed inappropriate. He pulled on the coffin cover, swinging it back into place. The temperature had dropped lower. Paul was beginning to shiver.

His mother would come. Maybe not his father. But his mother would find him. She had been a good mother, no matter how Paul had treated her. She would seek him out. Even if she had to search every cemetery in the city. Paul tried not to think of how many there were.

He rolled on his side and pulled his knees up as far as the little box would allow. How many months had passed? How cold had it become? Why had he been allowed to craft his own destiny?

Paul shivered. He was alone, just the way he had planned it.

The Soldiers' Home

Early mornings in the Firemen's Cemetery are notoriously shrouded in mist. Educated men might explain this by pointing out the land's elevation in relation to the nearest waterways as well as the role played by local weather. Those of a particular engineering bent would add the importance of Interstate 10 running along its western border. Spiritually minded men might suggest that regardless of such natural influences, these sacred grounds are a nexus wherein heaven and earth join, allowing the passing of so many souls that a certain residue is inevitably to be seen with the aid of the day's first sunlight.

The Fireman's Charitable and Benevolent Association had consecrated these grounds in the year 1852 and tourists might believe the more mischievous tour guides who spin tales of ghostly smoke and water-sprays from spectral hoses. The awkwardly dressed men with cameras enjoy the idea that firemen of old still battle it out with ancient fires for all eternity. Their wives tend to shudder at this image; some of them familiar with the dread of waiting for a husband to return from a hazardous job, and some simply burdened with an ingrained human alarm towards house fires.

Educated men scoff at notions of this kind and even spiritual men hesitate to give it credence. And in the end the tourists will tuck their photos away in a box along with the tour guide's fanciful tale and forget all about it. Neither the scholars, nor the religious, nor the tourists will ever understand just how close to the truth such tales do come.

Before the first ray of each new dawn, just as it seems as if the grip of night's darkness will never be broken, those who sleep lightly in the Fireman's Cemetery are disturbed by a muffled racket coming from a great, square society tomb. Standing along one open lane, deep within the field of the dead, it is rather plain in appearance, and by starlight is dreary looking—a heavy, squat figure resembling a rundown tenement or forgotten bureaucratic cellblock. Across the top edge of this monument, if the darkness were pulled away, one would see these words: Soldiers' Home.

A man's tired voice murmurs a few words, the only reply a sharp clank of metal on stone. Shuffling steps echo against the neighboring tombs, and then someone coughs. There is the sound of running followed by jeering laughter. A lower voice, wide and powerful, demands an answer. For the first time, distinct words are heard. "Yessir!"

Now, a great many footsteps can be heard. Rattling and clattering mix with coughing and veiled curses. It is evident that as many as ten or twenty men are moving about in the dark. If they are all of one purpose, it does not sound so. A short quarrel, muffled by the shroud of pre-dawn but no less violent than if it were conducted in sunlight, is cut short by a harsh command. The runner returns at the same time. Most of the clamor is now out on the open lane, in front of the Soldiers' Home. There is less noise, though a few more words are clearer now.

"Watch that," a husky voice warns.

"All right, all right." The lower voice concedes.

"Battery," a quick whisper. The last of the muted clanks and shuffles comes to an end.

All is silent now save for one figure who cannot stop coughing.

"Battery." This time, the voice carries more authority. The coughing stops for a breath, but begins anew.

The low voice issues an order. The coughing figure moves away from the others, back towards the dark block.

"Battery." There is no more noise. The black morning air holds for a collective pause.

The forms of men can now be seen as the first bit of grey is mixed into the atmosphere. There are four rows of men, five abreast, facing the Soldiers' Home. Before them stand two men, off to one side stands a thinner man. By their silhouettes, it is obvious that the men are standing at attention, arms held at their sides. Each man's head is covered by a misshapen cap. A few exceptions are bareheaded. All are uniformed, though most of the blouses ill fitting.

The thin man steps forward, facing the Battery. He bows his head and speaks.

"Our Father, which art in heaven..." his voice is as thin as his shadow.

The Battery joins in. The words of the prayer echo down the grassy lane, swallowed by the lingering night. When they finish, they are silent for a full minute.

From out of the Soldiers' Home comes the sound of a stifled cough.

"Detail." The word cuts the silence like an alarm, and the black forms break formation. Each line of men makes its way to one of the corners of the Soldiers' Home. Most of the black night has been replaced by a heavy gray that allows the men to be able to see shapes but nothing more. It is all that they need. Each corner of the blocked structure is composed of a cannon barrel standing on end. In the middle of the east and west walls stand two other cannon, though there are not enough men to work these. The men toil swiftly, their carefully plotted routine insuring that each cannon is lowered without injury to the men or damage to the stone artillery pieces.

As this is being done, two men from each detail pull open the nearest bottom vault and withdraw a stone cradle which will hold each great barrel. As their comrades set the cannons into the cradles, they already begin to withdraw bags of gunpowder, as well as the rammers, cleaning worms, sponges, lanyards, and friction primers. As one man seals each vent hole with his thumb, they first worm and swab out the barrels, removing any bits of masonry chips and dust that fell in during the process of removing the cannons from the monument. The vent holes are then cleaned out in the same manner. By the time the cannons are secured to the cradle, each team is ready to load their gun.

A bag of powder is rammed into place, and the brass friction primer is loaded into the vent hole. A stone cannon ball, from a stack on the monument's corners, is rammed into place. The five men now come to attention as one of them chuffs "Ready to fire!" One of the details is slow, and finishes ten seconds behind the others. An officer fidgets with his pocket watch.

"They'll make it, Colonel." The husky voice tries to reassure him.

"All right, all right." The Colonel's low voice betrays his aggravation.

"It's Vincent's men. There's only four of them. Theirs was the man with the cough."

"Yes, I know that, Major."

Enough light has crept into the field to allow the two officers to see facial expressions. The Colonel tries to smile. The strain is unmistakable even in the dim light.

"I don't like the men to be slack, Major. I was easy on them. Too easy. It's why we're all here."

"Begging your pardon, sir, but that's foolish. You're not to blame."

"Battery!" The Colonel's command cracks out sharply, ricocheting off the nearest crypts. The men stiffen, each gunner's hand grasping tightly to his lanyard.

"You know I'm right, sir. This melancholy of yours comes and goes. You'll think better of it. Just give it time." The Major gently touches his commanding officer's arm. "We've been over this hundreds of times."

The Colonel ignores the touch and the comforting words, staring instead at his pocket watch. He draws in a deep breath and then, without pause, barks:

"Fire!"

The four cannons belch smoke and thunder as well as stone chips and plaster dust. Quickly, as if their former lives depend on it, the men reload. Vincent's detail keeps up with the others and a second volley is fired. They fire a third and fourth volley as the smoke obliterates what little light the morning has to offer. Their world is no longer black. It is grey and white, the air thicker than the silk lining of the finest coffins.

"Shall they reload?" the Major asks. His men wait for his order. He steps closer to the Colonel in an attempt to see him clearly through the haze.

"Why do you always insist it is not my fault?" The Colonel snaps his pocket watch shut and rams it into his jacket. "I told Division they were ready. I volunteered them. Insisted they be sent forward. You call me a fool? Only a fool would deny me this judgment."

"The men, sir?" The Major waits for his Colonel's decision.

"Again, Major. They're off this morning. And the sick man is not to blame."

"Battery, reload!" The Major's shout lacks conviction and carries emotion he had hoped to keep hidden.

"Do not worry, Major. I know you disagree. You think I'm too hard on them."

"On yourself, sir."

The men are grimy with carbon, grout and sweat. The chalky residue from the stone guns is smeared across their faces, making them appear all the more ghostly. They work with determination, dragging out more bags of gunpowder, swabbing out the barrels, and ramming the loads in place. It is hot work. The cloying humidity, even in the early morning, attacks them. They press on, knowing there is no respite unless they improve. The Colonel has been known to push them until the late morning sun has finally forced them back into their graves. They fear this as much as they fear real combat. The sun is painful, and cuts deeply into their souls.

Yet, in the face of this toil and pain, they persevere. If they are ever to find peace, they know they must satisfy their Colonel. They must show him that his will has driven them beyond their limitations. That he has forced improvement upon them to such an extent that time can be reversed, they can be saved, and he can be redeemed. By his own sheer resolution he must drag them out of the pit that he himself dug for them.

He is demanding the impossible but they do not balk in the face of it. Yes, it is hard work. It is madness. But they soldier on.

"Fire!"

Smoke rolls in every direction. It filters down each adjacent lane, spreading its nauseating stench over and into tomb after tomb. Many of the dead, long used to this barrage, keep quietly in their crypts, content to wait out the Colonel's self-inflicted fury. On this day, there are no new arrivals to annoy him, demanding that he stop. The newest residents in the nearby crypts have already tried this and learned that the old soldier is as unmovable as Stonewall Jackson ever was. They will hate him for a long time. Eventually, as with the older dead, they will come to pity him.

"Cease fire!" The call is as loud and punishing as his earlier order to fire. And it does not mean the soldiers will now get their rest. Now they must move sharply, and attack the cannons in reverse, lifting the great barrels back into place, and stowing the cradles and tools without delay. If this is not done right, they may be forced to do it all over again. They work feverishly, both desiring to please their Colonel and fearful of his retribution.

"You see, Major, responsibility must rest somewhere. It cannot be passed along indefinitely. Even if it could, it should not be. Someone has to step in and take the weight of it. You must surely see that this is so."

The Major watches his men struggle to lift the stone cannons. In a way, his task is just as difficult. Just as repetitive. He has argued this point countless times. But he has never given in.

"Someone does take responsibility, Colonel. Someone of a much higher rank. You would not presume to make yourself His equal, would you?"

"Look closely at these vaults," the Colonel steps closer to the Soldiers' Home. The large memorial consists of five stacked rows of burial vaults. There are four vaults to each row. "As you are well aware, there are no names here. Only numbers. These men were destroyed beyond recognition. Twenty men on this side, twenty on the south side. Yet, we are only able to cobble together enough pieces to make twenty-four men. My God! I'll be damned if I'll stand for it."

The Colonel puts out a hand and leans heavily against a marble vault. His breaths are short and awkward.

"You insult your Superior by this proud obduracy." The Major is not moved by the Colonel's emotion. He once was long ago, but he has not been for a long time. He makes an effort to win the argument nonetheless. "Step aside, and admit your limitations. You are not God, and He never expected you to be one. There are times when other men's actions—even sins— affect us. We have no control over them. We simply do what we must and the end comes out all of its own accord."

The men of the Battery, constructed from the detritus of war, reassemble on the grassy lane, now at attention. Their eyes wide with the terror of expectancy. Their ears still ring with the cacophony of their exercise, they tremble with an excess of adrenaline. They only wait now to hear their commander's judgment.

The Colonel eyes them with weary assessment. He has seen them perform better. He knows it. They know it. But he is also aware they have done the best they could for that day. The larger question he must answer is whether or not it is enough.

"Step aside, you said?" the Colonel asks softly. "How that I wish I might."

He tugs at his buttoned collar and looks over the heads of his men. The smoke has spread out over the burial ground now, a white mist in the rays of the morning sun. The smoke will clear eventually, and the sun will burn them if they do not get under cover soon.

"Battery, fall out." His order is nearly a whisper, but the men hear it plainly enough. They break ranks and step out of the wide, grassy lane.

In the miasma of smoke and sunlight, the weary soldiers climb into their stone barracks, making little jokes as they go. They need rest. And at least for a day, they will get it.

"Thank you, Major. That will be all. For this day."

The Major disappears around one corner of the large tomb. His quarters are on the south side. Left alone, the Colonel stands erect as the smoke begins to clear. He endures the sunlight for a short time. It burns, and he imagines it is necessary.

"Not God." The Colonel chafes at the Major's impudence. "The man's got gall, I'll say that for him."

And then he is gone. The Colonel lies in his vault, just another corpse in a tomb that he has built with the power of his pride.

A cough is heard inside the Soldiers' Home. Then nothing more.

The sun rises. Early morning tourists remark upon the mist that lingers over the burial field. Another day begins.

What Scares Henry Payne

(*Danse Macabre 53*, Strontium)

There were twenty-three boys: fresh, clean-cut boys, who kept matching haircuts parted on their left side with washed necks red and exposed to the morning sun. Twenty-three young men of grace and fine education: of Homer and Hemingway, of ratios and rhombuses. Twenty-three little minds that could recite their times tables as accurately as their Whitman. Those lilacs blooming in the dooryard fit as neatly into their schedule as six times eleven and seven times eight. Ask any of the twenty-three boys, they would tell you: a rhombus has four sides, Homer came from Rome, Hemingway ended his drunken life with a bang. Bang! Twenty-two giggling boys.

The Hemingway joke never made Henry Payne laugh like the others. That's not the kind of thing that made Henry Payne laugh—a man's death. He never understood why the other boys laughed at such a thing. There was never anything funny about a man dying. In fact, Henry felt sure there was never anything a dead man might find funny; not once he'd figured out he was dead, not once he knew that everything he had ever planned to do would never come to pass.

"Stay together," a teacher with stiff blonde hair stood in the center of the open gates of Lafayette Cemetery Number One, her nose raised as if it pained her to hold her glasses in place.

A mocking chant from twenty-two boys arose. *Together! Together!* They pushed and shoved themselves into a tight mob. Twenty-two navy blue pullover oxfords with twenty-two crisp collars rubbed together to the sound of twenty-two students terribly pleased with themselves.

Henry Payne stood off to the side. Mrs. Simien was being overly protective, but he saw no reason to mock her. The scrum of boys rolled drunkenly towards him and he retreated three steps to avoid the crush.

"Mr. Payne!" Mr. Ansel, a thin man with a tweed blazer, grabbed him by the arm. "You heard Mrs. Simien. Keep with the group."

Henry looked at his raucous classmates and hesitated. He felt a sharp crack on the very top of his head and caught a fleeting glance of something in Mr. Ansel's hand. Mr. Ansel was known to carry a thick wooden ruler.

"Alright," Henry protested, rubbing his scalp. "Funny I should get smacked." He muttered this last bit while eyeing his unruly classmates.

A tour guide stood to one side, chatting with his cell phone while oblivious to the kids. His hair was long, tied in a loose ponytail. A thin, curly red beard acted as a poor sort of camouflage for his weak chin. Mrs. Simien having called to him several times, he flipped shut his phone and dropped it into one of the many large pockets running down the sides of his cargo pants.

"Boys!" Mrs. Simien tried to be stern. Her demand for order merely sounded shrill and annoying.

Henry stayed near the back of the group. The tour guide was soft spoken and Henry could hear very little of what he said. He did not care. Nothing about the crypts and their occupants interested him. He watched the tour guide with indifference. As he did, a tall, square-shouldered boy stepped into his line of sight and made eye contact. Henry wanted to turn away. The tall boy, Edward Matthews, was always trouble. Henry did turn away, but only after looking into Edward's eyes, and only then very slowly.

The tour continued: row after row of crypts, coping tombs, and monuments. Henry tried to fall further behind the group. Once, Mr. Ansel made a lazy attempt to hit him with the wooden ruler but missed. The attempt did not deter Henry. By the midway point of the tour, Henry had escaped.

Neither Mrs. Simien nor Mr. Ansel noticed Henry's absence. Billy Cuthbert did, watching Henry drift farther and farther away. Billy was the closest thing to a friend Henry had found in school. When he saw Henry slip around the backside of a large, crumbling family crypt, Billy followed.

"Whatcha doin'?" Billy playfully poked a finger into Henry's back. Henry spun around, his eyes shifting.

"You're gonna get me in trouble." Henry stated this as fact.

"Am not."

Both boys knew Mr. Ansel was on the other side of the crypt, looking for soft white flesh to whack.

Henry moved down the grassy aisle, ignoring a grand, red granite crypt that dominated everything near it. Billy, smaller than Henry, had to add an extra step or two to keep up. They moved in silence, each boy occasionally looking at his companion. It was a simple gesture understood by boys around the world—I'm right here, not going anywhere. As verbally driven as boys can instinctively be, there comes that moment when the need to speak is gone, as if all the words have been said and anything added would be a waste of time. Billy kept two steps behind Henry.

Billy was a wide-eyed boy. Pale skin and a white blond hairline sitting high on his forehead gave him a queer albino look. His short fine hair did not stand up, as it should have, instead staying plastered against his scalp as if it were perpetually wet. This only exaggerated his pasty appearance. Both elbows and knees bent at awkward angles, and he walked as if he knew it, sheepishly tucking his elbows as far back as practical and minimizing his stride to limit the bend of his knees. He managed all of this while keeping himself tilted slightly forward.

"You lookin' for somethin'?" Billy felt as if he had to whisper.

Henry ignored him.

"You runnin' from you-know-who?" Billy said this a little louder. Henry glanced sharply in his direction. Billy nodded. "Yeah, I saw him givin' you that look. But he ain't followin'."

"Go back to the class, Billy." Henry sped up, trying to create distance between them. Billy had only to hop an extra step or two to keep up.

"Hey!" Billy jammed on the brakes and sounded as if he'd been stung by a wasp. He stared alarmingly at the faceplate of a crypt. His pale face, lit by the glaring sun, was difficult to read but his nervous stance made his discomfort clear. "Look'it that."

His bony white finger aimed at a row of eroded letters in the crypt's marble. Henry, wishing to move on, could not ignore the strange tone in the boy's voice. He turned back and stepped up to the plate.

"See it?" Billy tried to swallow but his throat was too dry.

"I see some old names. Why?"

"Look—right under that one. You don't see that?"

"Some guy who died over a hundred and fifty years ago. What about him?" Henry wiped sweat from his eyes and wondered what had come over his uninvited companion.

"Henry," Billy said with force, "Henry Payne. Have you gone blind? Don't you see it says *Henry Payne* on that tombstone?"

Henry read the name two or three times before acknowledging Billy. The letters were worn and the name was not easy to read. But Henry could see it clearly enough. He reached out and touched his name with the tip of a finger. Almost any other time, he would have noticed his name immediately. Even if it had only been the first name, it would have leapt out at him. Like most young people, Henry was still at that age when he was easily caught off guard seeing his first name where he did not expect it; that mixture of guilt, surprise, and a small confirmation to the conceited adolescent mind of self-importance. But despite this, he had not really seen his name on the crypt plate. The fact intrigued him. He pressed his fingertip into the grooves of the capital H, sensing that if he pushed it hard enough he could smudge it out. He had the distinct feeling it was as soft as dough and his name could simply be rubbed away.

"I don't like that—your name on that tomb." Billy wished Henry would stop touching it. "I don't like that at all."

"It ain't my name, Billy. Just some guy who died a long time ago."

"Well, I know that." Billy leaned forward, drawn to the letters as Henry had been, but he couldn't actually bring himself to touch them. "I know it ain't your name. But you gotta admit that feels wrong, you know? That don't give you shivers? That don't scare ya, seein' your name on that grave?"

Henry turned and looked at Billy with a silent shake of his head.

"Scares *me*," Billy said, "and it ain't even my name."

"Dead ain't something to be afraid of." Henry's gaze drifted over the rows of crypts. "Nothin' dead scares me."

"Easy to say with the sun shinin'," Billy eyed the neighboring crypts with unease. "I just think seein' your name on there reminds me how one day we'll all die. Only this is like a spotlight on you—*Henry Payne is going to die.*"

"You about done? 'Cause nothing you've said scares me. Don't bother me t'all."

Henry turned his back on the crypt of dead Henry Payne and walked boldly away. He lifted his head as if to let Billy Cuthbert know he was as opposite of scared as he could be. The fact was, while it had surprised him, seeing his name really *did not* scare him. He even felt a certain sense of curiosity—something compelling him to learn what would eventually be the deciding factor of his death.

"You don't fool me, Henry Payne. I know what you're really afraid of. I could see it in your eyes jus' a few minutes ago. You're afraid of *him*." Billy was still shaken from seeing Henry's name on the front plate and found that taunting Henry took some of the edge off his nerves. "You're afraid of Eddie Matthews!"

Henry stopped walking. He took a deep breath and exhaled as if afraid to disturb the air around him. He cocked his head to one side and said nothing.

"You ain't gotta act like that, Henry. Heck, we're all scared of Eddie Matthews. Don't look so upset about it."

"You don't know nothin'. You don't know nothin' at all. Why don't you just go back with that pack of wild dogs." The yelps and bayings of their group could be heard growing nearer. "You fit in just fine with that lot. Leave me alone."

"Hey," Billy's voice became tender, "I was only pickin' at ya. I know all about Eddie Matthews. I know what he's done. Eddie talks too much, ya know? He was telling the guys all about how he caught you in the garage just before Christmas break. How he knocked you down on the oily floor—smashed your face into the concrete. I know what he did. Ain't no reason to act 'shamed."

Henry's eyes reddened as Billy spoke. It was evident he had not been aware that others knew about the garage. Tears formed in his eyes and he concentrated on not blinking. *Never show. Never show.* Henry repeated the phrase over and over, the mantra he had learned at home. *Never show my pain.* The words deadened him like a soporific spell.

"Most of the guys are on your side." Billy tried to calm Henry down. "Wasn't nobody really thought Eddie was right for what he did. He's a creep. He shouldn'tuv hurt you like that. And I can see why you're afraid of him."

Tightening his jaw, Henry silently mouthed the words—*Never show. Never, never show.*

"You're right, of course. This old place ain't got nothin' to be scared of. There ain't no dead things to be scared of. Just people. It's the damn people that are alive that scare the guts out of ya. Eddie scares me." Billy's pale face grew paler as he spoke. "You know what? When Eddie was tellin' that story about the garage, and he said he squeezed them channel locks— well I'm sorry Henry. I was just thinkin' how glad I was it was you and not me. I mean, I just was relieved it wasn't my skin gettin' smashed like that. I'd never been so glad you had all the good grades. I ain't proud of that.

But I was afraid, and it wasn't even happenin' to me. So I'm just sayin' you don't need to be 'shamed of being scared."

"I'm not scared of Eddie Matthews." Henry trembled as the words formed on his lips. "That's not what scares me."

"Come on, Henry. You ain't got to be so tough."

"What else do I have to say?" Henry stepped up to Billy with clenched fists. He was visibly shaking. "Can't you hear me? I'm not scared of him—he's not the one that scares me! Now leave me alone!"

Henry ran down the grassy lane and turned, disappearing between two crumbling crypts. Billy did not follow. He stood still for a few moments, then headed for the sounds of his other classmates.

It did not matter to Henry what Billy did. He was not thinking of the pale boy, though his taunts remained. He hadn't wanted to think of that garage: the smell of oil, the cool grit of the old cement pressing his cheek, or the tearing grip of the rusted channel locks on soft flesh. He could hear Eddie's cruel and hungry laughter. See the excitement in his eyes. Henry shut out the memory. Pushed it away—pulled at it like a desperate man fighting to unwrap the constricting coils of a python. If he failed, if he could not fight it down, he knew the suffocation awaiting him. Knew the darkness that would envelope him. A pitch-black hunger lusting for him. It had nearly devoured Henry in the garage. Since then, he had lived with the knowledge that he could never defeat it again. He believed in this certainty. He bore the strictest faith in its inevitability, even to the point of accepting he would never make the slightest effort to fight it.

Eddie's laughter rang out closer than memory should have allowed. Henry jammed his heels into the freshly cut grass and stood rock still. The laughter was no memory. Henry did not have the luxury of hearing a memory he could banish through the will of a strong mind. The laughter was real. It was coming from the mouth of Edward Matthews. He was standing only a few steps away.

"You in a hurry like the Devil's on yer tail." Eddie smiled with gleaming straight teeth. "Too bad you got nowhere t'be."

"Go 'way. Please." Henry's eyes opened wide. His breathing became shallow. He looked as if the python were already compressing his chest. "Get out of here, Eddie."

"Not so tough today, huh? You and that brave face in the garage. Like you could take it. Not then, and not now. I taught you a lesson, dint I? Taught ya who's scary. Who you can't beat with that snotty brain of yours. Now you know it don' matter how smart you are—or how polite and polished up you act. Don' mean a thing. It's useless when it bumps heads with big scary things. I see it in your eyes, Henry Payne. All your fancy playactin' is up against what you can't beat—me."

Eddie pulled a screwdriver from his back pocket, rolling it with his fingers. He watched its Phillips head scatter crisscross patterns in the sun.

"On your knees, hotshot." Eddie grasped the handle of the screwdriver as if it were a knife.

"You were close, Eddie." Henry focused on the tip of the screwdriver, barely able to draw breath. "I did learn who I'm afraid of. I did learn all my books and upbringing couldn't fight the one I'm afraid of. Yeah, I'm afraid. Terrified. Don't do this. *Please*. You're wrong about what scares me."

"I said get on your knees," Eddie extended his arm and jammed the screwdriver into Henry's kneecap. Henry grunted in pain but stood his ground. His eyes clouded over, as if he'd been wrapped in a black shroud.

"You ain't just a little wrong—you're all wrong. I ain't afraid of you."

Henry reached up with cold, deliberate calculation and stripped the screwdriver from Eddie's hand. Without breaking rhythm, he spun the tip of the gleaming tool and drove it into Eddie's ribs. Eddie whimpered in shock.

"You see what scares me?" Henry rammed Eddie against a faux-marble crypt, dislodging a loose stone. Eddie sucked in a wet, bubbling breath.

Henry had been right. The blackness had overcome him before he could even fight it. He could not stop it. He wouldn't stop it. He had given up wrestling with that serpent he had first met on the floor of a garage. With each thrust of the screwdriver, Henry could feel the python clamping ever more tightly. And it seemed as if it would never stop.

What point in wrestling with it? All the books in Henry Payne's canon could not define the beast that had slithered from its lair. And no amount of discipline could supply enough oxygen to overcome its stranglehold on him. Not one of his teachers had ever told him such a beast had ever existed, though he was acutely aware that his ignorance could not explain away the bloody corpse of Eddie Matthews. And no cop, judge, or jury would ever acknowledge the beast's complicity in Henry's crime, nor the existence of their own hidden monsters.

Twenty-one boys walked out of Lafayette Cemetery Number One: fresh, clean-cut boys, who kept matching haircuts that parted on their left side with washed necks red and exposed to the late morning sun. Twenty-one young men of grace and fine education: of politics and Poe, of restraint and rage. Twenty-one little men, unaware of what lay deeply buried beneath their twenty-one navy blue pullover oxfords.

The Dream Monger

The tragedy of life is not death, but what we let die inside us while we live.

--Norman Cousins

There was nothing festive about this first death. No matter that we were in New Orleans. There were no jazz musicians to march us to the tombs. No bold speeches about a party on the Golden Streets. No audacious suggestion that the recently deceased was in a better place. There was no music at all. Nothing to say. Three college friends were meeting after twenty-five years on a cold, rain soaked morning beside a whitewashed tomb in St. Louis Cemetery Number Three. Two of us stood shivering without umbrellas, stunned that the third lay enclosed in a cheap wooden coffin.

"I spoke with him last year," Dave said defensively.

I hadn't spoken to the dead man for at least three years so I said nothing in reply.

"Chip hadn't changed much, you know. Still full of ideas. Still planning to set the art world on its ear." Dave pinched the rain collecting at the end of his nose and tried to smile. His grotesque smile reminded me of a garishly colored Mardi Gras mask. "Yeah, Chip hadn't changed a bit. Good old Chip."

"Yeah," I said quietly. I didn't mean it. I really wanted to call him a liar. The last time I had seen Charles he'd been a drunken failure. And why was Dave still calling him Chip? Charles had dropped that idiotic moniker before we had even graduated. God, but that was twenty years ago. I said none of this to Dave. I couldn't really see the point.

The priest finished his litany. The rain stopped falling only moments after. I was more relieved that the priest had shut up. I had been able to ignore the rain. Even though I couldn't remember a word of Latin, it had depressed the hell out of me.

We stared in silence as two ragged looking caretakers shoved the coffin onto the top tier of the open tomb. That's all there was—that one long gravelly scrape of the coffin along the edge of the wet stone shelf. Workers would brick up the opening later in the day and smear a coat of mortar over it. One of them would etch the date in the mortar and Charles would not see the light of day for at least one year and one day. At the end of that period all bets were off. I wondered if he had any relatives who might join him next year but couldn't remember much about his family. Maybe he'd been the last one. Maybe there'd be no one left to tend the family tomb and keep it from falling into desuetude. I toyed with the idea that I might return occasionally on All Saints Day and give it the care it would need but I knew otherwise. I had never visited him consistently while he had been alive. Why would I now that he was dead?

Dave wanted to leave. He didn't say that. He didn't have to. I watched the Priest from the corner of my eye as he walked quietly away. Dave took a step in the same direction, but only one. He could tell I wasn't moving and made an exaggerated effort to assure me I should take all the time I needed. Patronizing bastard. What did he care about Charles? Charles had stolen at least two girlfriends from Dave. I really shouldn't have judged Dave. At least he'd made the trip. Maybe he just wanted to see Charles entombed. Maybe he actually enjoyed it.

So why hadn't the fourth man in our group made an appearance? I hadn't made an effort to visit Charles in years; Dave had an axe to grind with Charles. Neither one of us had a very good reason to come and witness the burial. But the fourth man should have come. He should have been the one to see that Charles was given the proper respect. I should not have been the one standing in front of that tomb. Neil should have been standing in my place.

I asked Dave if he had heard from Neil. Dave, still yearning to flee, stepped away again, then back in my direction.

"Neil? Neil Everett?"

I looked around to see who was speaking. A leathery man just shorter than the both of us was leaning on the corner of a grey tomb whose steeple pointed defiantly at the sky. He was wearing a suit of the same color as the tomb behind him. I had never seen him before. I would wish I had ignored him.

"Do you know Neil?" Dave asked the stranger.

It was an absurd question. I couldn't say why but it was obvious he could know very little about our friend.

"I'm sorry about Charles." The stranger nodded towards Charles' tomb. "He was quite the dreamer."

"You knew Charles too?"

I wanted Dave to shut up. I wanted him to stop asking questions. I wanted this interloper to go away.

"I only knew Charles through Neil." The man pushed off from the tomb and came near to us. I wanted to back away from him but I knew Charles' tomb was directly behind me and there would be no way to move off to the side without making an obvious retreat. "I'm John. John Smith."

Dave reached out and shook his hand. I did nothing of the kind. John Smith? What kind of joke was that?

"Are you here to sell us something?" I didn't really mean it. I was simply attempting to offend him and run him off.

"I don't sell. I buy." He looked into my eyes and I had to turn and look down the wide empty lane between the tombs. There were a few people there, actually, but they were far away; tourists, judging by their over-large yellow and purple t-shirts.

"What do you buy?" Dave asked. I wanted to punch Dave on the jaw to shut him up.

As if he could read my mind, John Smith looked sideways at me with cold eyes as he handed Dave a small card. Dave read it before handing it to me. I reluctantly took it.

Smith's name was in bold letters in the center of the card. Under that, in smaller print, it read: Dream Monger. And below that: Peace of Mind—Reasonable Rates.

A late raindrop landed dead in the center of the card, soaking and distorting the printed words.

"What does this mean?" I asked.

"Did you know Charles wanted to be more than just an artist?" asked the smug John Smith.

"No." Dave just wouldn't keep quiet.

"He wanted to be an artist, you know that much. But once he had achieved greatness, he wanted to go to Paris, or Milan, and discover new talent that he could cultivate and present to the world."

"I never heard him talk about that," Dave said, as if he were ashamed to discover there were things he did not know about Charles.

I hadn't known it either, but I didn't care. It sounded like more of Charles' romantic hogwash. I'd grown tired of that not long after I'd met him.

"How did you know what Charles wanted?" Dave stepped towards Charles' tomb and caressed its side. I got the feeling he was about to bend forward and kiss it. If he had I would have cursed him for the stupid fool he was and never spoken to him again.

"Dreams are my business. It's my business to know a man's dreams. And like I said, I met Charles through Neil." The stranger wiped gently at the beads of rain sprinkled across his coat. "Neil was not much of a dreamer, which was both a blessing and curse for me. He was easy to do business with, but I did not end up with much of a deal."

He was right about Neil. Neil had never been one to spend his days chasing down a dream. He always seemed content to watch the rest of us pursue our dreams. But no matter how intuitive John Smith was regarding my friends, I didn't like it. The man had no business passing judgment—no matter how fair and accurate—on any of us.

"Charles was a different matter," John Smith continued. I could tell by his eyes he knew he was irritating me. "Charles had the kind of dreams that continue to get bigger regardless of a man's ability to catch them. In fact, it seemed that for every year that passed, Charles grew more and more dependent on his dreams. Such dreams can become priceless, magical. They're almost too wonderful to describe. But, as is often the case with such things, I came out on the wrong end of that deal. To be honest, your friends did not do me any favors. I did Neil a favor. And I tried to do Charles a favor."

"Let's get out of here, Dave." I looked at the wet tombs surrounding us and knew we shouldn't be talking with this man. He was wasting our time, and probably out of his mind. I had no desire to find out he was on the level. I felt unclean even considering it.

"What favor did you do for Neil?" Dave's question was laughably predictable.

"I bought his dreams from him, of course." John Smith studied Dave with eyes that would not stay still. "It's what I do. I freed Neil of his dreams and gave him contentment. *Peace of Mind* is more than worth the value of a dream."

"I don't believe you. Neil wouldn't do that." Dave was hardly convincing.

"You don't understand, do you?" John Smith crossed lightly to Charles' tomb and rapped it with his cane. "Who should have been here to see Charles off? Neil was a closer friend than either one of you. But he's not here, is he? Where is he, then?"

Dave's eyes met mine and I knew we were thinking the same thing. Neither one of us had been a friend to Charles for a very long time. And, like him or not, John Smith was right. Neil should have been there.

"Neil didn't come because he has no need to be here." John Smith smiled at us as if we were children who had misunderstood a simple truth. "He has no more romantic notions of past friendships. He is content to know these friendships are over. He doesn't try to hold on to them. Peace of mind is enough for him."

"I'm going, Dave." I touched his shoulder. It was meant to be a friendly and comforting gesture but it felt more like I was just pushing him out of my way.

"He doesn't understand, Dave." John Smith's cold smile held me in place. "Let him go. I'm not here to do business with him. This fool gave up his dreams without even securing something in return. All the anxiety and none of the hope. But you, Dave, are a different story."

I should have left. I wanted to. I didn't.

"He's a common breed, actually," Smith glared in my direction while still addressing Dave. "Most people don't have dreams strong enough to buy. The average man's dreams are tissue-paper-like affairs that tear and break up when the first tear soaks into them. Most people have already discarded them before I get a chance at them. I don't mind. Dreams like that have no value to me."

"Don't listen to him." I grew angrier at every word Smith spoke. "He's lying. Charles wouldn't sell his dreams. You know that."

"I never said he did sell them, young man." Smith turned on me with predatory eyes. "Do you want to know why Charles died? Hmm? He refused to sell me his dream and it *overwhelmed* him. Smothered the poor bastard. The whole thing was silly. He didn't have the talent to fulfill his dream. But he clung to it like it meant something. But in the end he simply died of a broken heart. A pointless death. Dave doesn't need to live like that—or die like that. His dreams, what little they are, aren't worth the trouble. Sell them to me, and he gets his money's worth of contentment."

"What do you get out of this? What do you do with my dream?" Dave's voice sounded like a little boy's.

"That's my business, son. Not yours," he flashed a smile, white teeth gleaming like the rows of sepulchers around us. "If you're worried about it going to a good home—don't. Once we complete the transaction, it is of no concern to you thereafter."

It was an easy thing to snatch the cane out of Smith's hand and crack him over the head. He'd been leaning on it, and lost his balance, his head hitting the corner of the stone base of Charles' family crypt. He made no noise. All I heard was the clatter of the cane as I dropped it on the paved walkway.

"What'd ya do that for?" Dave gaped.

"This old man's crazy. We need to get out of here." It helped to say it aloud. I repeated it several more times for good measure. "The man's crazy."

"You selfish—what do you know about him? Who says he's crazy?"

"I do." I walked away, but stopped when I realized Dave had not followed. Turning, I watched Dave kneel beside Smith's limp body. "Forget this guy, okay? He's a lunatic."

"I guess so," Dave hovered doubtfully over him. "I'm just gonna stay here and make sure he's okay. That's all I'm gonna do. Go on without me."

I could have forced him to leave with me. But I didn't see the point. I could feel the anger in me rising and I had to get out of that graveyard and back to my life.

I knew I hated Smith for presuming to know so much about us. But I hated him more for being right. Somewhere along the way, I had tossed my dreams aside for a cup of coffee, or maybe only a stick of gum. But at least I hadn't sold them to Smith. And they were still out there, if I could ever find them again, hidden away in some old desk drawer or under a pile of outdated magazines. I might have set them aside once, but just watching Smith lust after Dave's dreams made me protective of something that had meant nothing to me for almost twenty years.

As friends in college we had faced all things life had to offer. Or so we had imagined. But we had never faced death. We had shared many things: pain, passion, youth, and hope. A few of us had even shared a girlfriend or two. They had been heady days of dreams and expectations; four souls hell-bent on crashing through heaven's gates costumed as little gods of a great big world.

But little gods die.

The Rossi

(*Danse Macabre 54*, Lagniappe)

"What does he want?" I asked, as the pompous looking stiff in the ruffled shirt slunk away from our crypt. Like I had to ask.

"He's harmless, Jim. Just lonely. He died a long time ago, and his wife is still *out there*. He's just lonely."

My wife had a knack for stating the obvious.

"How can his wife still be alive?" I did the math. The fop must have been sixty when he'd died, and he'd been interred for thirty or forty years. "Was he married to an infant?"

"You're not funny, dear. And don't ever say that in front of him. It still hurts him very much." Greta tilted her head, a sure sign she was fighting back empathetic tears. "You never had to wait for me. Be thankful, and gracious as well."

I knew where this was going and tried to change the subject.

"It's been too long since the kids have come to visit."

"I wonder," she continued, not about to be swayed by my ruse, "how you would have handled being here without me?"

"I would have managed." I wasn't claustrophobic by nature, but there were times the crypt pressed in on me so hard that I could have sworn we were buried under six feet of compacted earth like damned Yankees. When I thought of what might have happened if I had died first, the imagined weight of that dirt was unbearable.

"You would have worried yourself into a second death. For the first time in your life, you would have been unable to protect me and care for me. It would have destroyed you."

"That might be." *Might be?* I would have shredded my fingers and bones, tearing down the cemetery walls. I would have found a way to get back to her. If not, I wouldn't have been cold six months before some deadbeat would have wormed his way into her life and tried to steal her away.

"Let's be honest, dear. You would have gone insane in this crypt, desperate to get back to me." Her laughter wasn't light-hearted. It stank of condescension.

"Don't be ridiculous. Or insulting."

"I'm just trying to make you see why Mr. Mouton is so lonely. Maybe I understand him better. After all, I had to wait for you."

"First of all, Mr. Mouton doesn't bother anyone other than you. If he's so lonely, he's perfectly free to haunt someone else's wife. And secondly, if his wife had the good manners to lie down and die like I had, he wouldn't have to wait so long. She's probably gone and latched onto some other poor old bastard. Probably doesn't even remember her dead husband."

"You're unusually cruel tonight." Greta tried to soothe me as if I were an overly excited child. "Why do you let things like this distract you?"

"*Let* things? This isn't my fault. Unless you want me to physically restrain the man from visiting you." I had to admit that wasn't a bad idea. I wasn't sure it was possible for a spirit to restrain another spirit, but it might be fun to give it a try.

"That wasn't what I meant." Whispering, she sounded as if she were afraid our neighbors might hear us. The idea was absurd.

On the southern side of us, the Métiers made so much noise, they could never hear anyone outside their own family vault. There must have been thirty of those idiots crammed into their shabby brick hut. Across from us, three dilapidated tombs could barely keep from falling into one another. No one had taken up residence in any of them for over one hundred years. The original inhabitants hadn't been seen or heard from by any one presently residing in our section of St. Louis Number Three. The lot behind us was empty, save for the unkempt thatch of grass and thistle that no living man would deign to wrestle into submission.

As for the crypt to the north, it really didn't matter if anyone there could hear us. It wasn't abandoned. Every two to ten years, a new arrival would slide through its front door. Their stele listed twenty-one names. They were all in there. No one had ever seen them leave. But never, at least in the fifteen years since I'd been interred, had anyone from the Rossi crypt so much as said *boo*. As dead people went, they gave me the creeps.

"Well?" I made an effort *not* to lower my voice. We had whispered enough in life, always trying to keep the kids from overhearing our quarrels. "What did you mean?"

"You're looking for something to worry about. You aren't happy unless you're worried."

"That doesn't make sense." It wasn't the first time she had made such a suggestion. And it wasn't the last time it wouldn't make sense. "I'm not making this stuff up. You know I'm not. Mr. Mouton shows far too much interest in you. And he's not the only one."

"I can't help that," she said, twisting her wedding and engagement rings back and forth. "I never encourage them."

"Right." And she was right, in a way. She never consciously encouraged men to fall in love with her. In the same way the flame made no conscious effort to attract the moth. She was simply who she was. A bright, shining, warm fire in the cold darkness of death. She had been the same in life.

"Don't be sarcastic. I can't help that my kindness is misconstrued."

"Okay, I'll do my best. And maybe you can do your best not to begrudge my caution and vigilance. I spent a lifetime stepping between you and every oddball you attracted. Don't expect me to quit now."

"What is it with me and strange men? Why do all the nuts want to attach themselves to me? There must be something wrong with me."

"Greta, dear, how many times do I have to say this? Normal, well-balanced men fell for you all the time, they were simply too well-balanced to embarrass you by showing it. It was only the kooks who showed themselves."

"That explains your unbalanced jealousy. And your willingness to show it."

"You know," I let out a long sigh in order to calm down and keep from making an ass of myself, "I never could figure out when it was I switched from playing the role of your White Knight to that of your jailor. I wish I knew the exact time. It would give me a definite moment in time at which I could hurl my curses."

"I just wish you'd stop *being* my jailor." It did not matter that she was whispering again. The words, long unspoken, rang out across the city of corpses like cathedral bells tolling the names of the dead. *Here, in this crypt, lies the cold, ashen remains of a long, dead love.*

Until that day I had puzzled over our existence in that gray world of the earthly dead. But no longer did it puzzle me. We were in Hell.

We avoided each other, as much as we could in that stone cell. I retreated to the lower depths, amidst the dusty memories of my ancestors. Ours was not a crowded tomb, like our southern neighbors. I had few family members, most of whom were still on the outside. My father and a few of my uncles were overseas, amongst the glorious battalions of dead heroes in Normandy. I could only hope they were doing better than I.

There were scant traces left of my older ancestors, deep in the *caveau*. Those few who could communicate never did. They had never known me in life, and that seemed to suit them just fine. I didn't care. I kept to myself and never bothered them.

Greta did not leave. I did not know if that was by choice or not. For all I knew she was bound to our crypt by a tie far stronger than the marriage document that had bound us in life. There had been no rules, no solid explanations for anything that we were experiencing. So she stayed, spending most of her time on the steps of our crypt.

I often heard her up there, speaking softly to passers-by. I kept an ear out for old Mouton, but he did not come as often as before. Maybe she had warned him off. Maybe he could simply sense that he should keep his distance. I was just glad he had backed off.

And then one night I thought I heard her speaking to Mouton again, and it took a second night of their conversation before I realized this was a *new* male voice. By the third night, I had decided to ascend long enough to see who was befriending my wife.

He was lithesome, something I never was and always resented in other men; a handsome man in a custom-tailored suit. I hated him right away. And then I discovered why, and I not only hated him, but feared him as well.

"Jim," Greta's introduction was stiff; she was hesitant for us to meet, "this is Mr. Rossi."

He nodded. I openly stared at him. He would not look me in the eye, backing away with an inaudible excuse. I continued to stare until he slipped into the Rossi crypt. I'd never felt death to such a degree from anyone else in that graveyard save from this one man.

"Where the hell did he come from?" It was not a frivolous question.

"Don't start," Greta was nearly in tears. "Dominic came just a few days ago."

"Oh, I can tell he's new. And he obviously hasn't read the memo from his forefathers yet. Did you explain to him that the Rossi don't mingle with us common dead?"

"No one's there."

"No one's where?"

"The Rossi crypt. It's empty." She winced as she said it, as if she were afraid of my reaction. Did she think I'd accuse her of lying? Not her. But someone else.

"And he's lonely, is that it?"

It was her turn not to look into my eyes.

"For what it's worth," I said, knowing I would be ignored even as I spoke, "you should stay away from him. He's wrong. He's very wrong. Wrong enough that even you should see it."

When she finally made eye contact, I wished that she hadn't. I could see the distrust and cold resistance pooled in those eyes and I retreated back into the depths of our dead, stone house.

He came every night. I could hear them speaking in lowered tones. Every once in a while I would slip up to the crypt door and listen to them. He was too smooth for his own good. He had traveled much in the living world and more recently than any of us. He had much to say and Greta hung on his every word.

I was almost ready to concede that I'd been wrong about him until the night he offered to show

Greta the Rossi crypt. Even Greta knew how strange his offer sounded. She hadn't forgotten everything I'd taught her.

"That's kind of you, but I'd rather not." She hated refusing anyone anything. But she had wisely said no.

Good girl, I almost said aloud. I descended to my room, taking with me the first bit of satisfaction I'd been able to latch onto in a long, long time.

Maybe I really had acted childishly. At least in my distrust of Dominic Rossi. There was no doubt I was jealous of his current knowledge of the living world. His sophistication threatened me as well. This was a vanity of mine that had carried over from my days when I had still drawn breath. Greta had always scolded me for it. Had said I was certainly sophisticated enough. *Enough*. Comments like that only complicated the issue.

At first I did not recognize the scream. I had never, in my living years or in the years since, heard my wife scream. Not really scream. And yet after that first moment of confusion, I *knew* it was her. Greta was screaming.

Bursting from our crypt, I scanned the dark night that surrounded me. I did not know how late it was, but there were no other spirits visible up or down our lane. The only other souls other than my own were Greta's and Dominic Rossi's. And what I could see of them chilled the vapor of my soul until it nearly condensed into a tangible, sodden horror.

Dominic Rossi held one arm around Greta's waist, tugging her from behind. He had wrapped his other arm around her right arm as she struggled to reach behind and scratch at him. So violent and quick was this action that I had no time to wonder how he could actually hold and restrain her. I only knew she was under his control and I feared I would be physically unable to interfere.

He backed up until his boots hit the base of the Rossi Crypt. Staring at me, no expression on his face, he rammed a shoulder against the stele of the crypt which gave in as if it were a door on a hinge. I understood then, as clearly as if a voice from heaven called down to me, that if he managed to gain the threshold with her and slam shut that entrance, I would never be able to reach my Greta again.

I dashed forward with the speed of hurricane force winds. Greta, seeing me, reached out her free hand to me, terror in her eyes. The scream I'd heard had become a painful roar as she called my name.

And then the stele plate slammed shut with a furious stone crash. I felt my spirit fall as I imagined Greta's fate. But I was amazed to discover that I had not been barred from the Rossi Tomb. I was, by some miraculous act, standing inside the blackness of that crypt. I could see nothing, but I had not been kept out, and that was all that mattered.

I wasted no time marveling at how this had occurred. I pushed forward blindly, my spirit slipping along twisted stone corridors that led down through the tomb. There were no steps, only slanted cold paths slick with mildew and mold. I traveled long enough to know that I could no longer be in the Rossi crypt, nor could I be in the sacred soil of our St. Louis Cemetery. Surely we had crossed below Esplanade, or had we in fact turned north and travelled deep under City Park? Clearly we had crossed some border into regions I dared not contemplate. Or had we? It was possible that my panic and fright had deluded me, filling my soul with twisted scenes that could not have possibly been true.

Twice I stepped on something like a small body, but the second time, I did not retract my foot in fear. I held it over the squirming mass long enough to realize it was slithering along the edge of the tunnel. Though I had wanted a light, I was suddenly thankful of the darkness. Pressing to the far side of the passage, I hurried on, forcing down my revulsion at whatever slid along beside me.

A harsh, keening cry rose out of a crevice that branched off the main passage. The crevice was impossible to see, but it stank of ancient rot and cold air poured from it in great blasts. I shielded myself against it and pressed beyond it. I hated to think that Greta had been exposed to this terrifying avenue. Yet, she had, and I knew she was not far ahead of me.

Something splashed against the back of my hand and I quickly swiped at it. It clung to me like bile. I reached out in the darkness and scuffed my hand against the stone walls, scratching and tearing away the offensive mucus.

And then light—low reddish light—began to glow ahead of me. I redoubled my effort to rush on.

Wherever we ended up, whatever really happened, it made no difference when I caught up with my wife's abductor. For when I did, we faced off in a stone cavity that was not much bigger than our own crypt. Greta was just beyond my reach, and the Rossi devil still clung to her like sin. A harsh red glare lit the chamber.

His right hand was no longer at her waist. It was, instead, wrapped around her throat. I held back, trembling as I looked for a chance to liberate her.

"Have you gone mad?" I demanded of him. "Are you the devil, himself?"

"I'm neither!" he declared, a surprising whine in his voice. "Don't take her from me. I can't be alone anymore! I won't be!"

Greta no longer struggled against him, but I could see how frightened she was and I fought the urge to bull-rush them and take the chance that I could free her.

"You may not be *the* devil, but you *are* one," I hissed.

"You can't understand." He jerked Greta to the right and shot a look into the darkness over his shoulder.

I gave my attention to the same vicinity of the chamber and noticed that another open doorway gave access to yet another corridor leading ever down.

"Don't take her through there," I beseeched him. "Don't go any lower!"

"Don't go lower?" His voice bounced around the chamber like a chorus of lunatics. "It's you who made me bring her this deep! Why did you follow us? Why have you chased us into these damned passages?"

"What are they?" I asked. "Where are we?"

"Where do you think? I found them as soon as I was rammed into this hellhole. I couldn't believe I was alone. Where had the rest of the Rossi gone? I should have found my family. Instead, there was no one!"

I kept my eyes on his fingers as they held tight to Greta's neck. They tightened then relaxed in erratic patterns, and I could not decide if I should jump in and try to wrest her away from him. I hoped talking would calm him.

"These passages? You found them? Where do they lead?"

"You can't seriously ask that question? They lead down, always down. And all of my family has gone by this path. At first I wondered why, but as I languished under my loneliness, I began to understand. I began to realize that going *there* had to be better than this horrifying loneliness. Can't you see that? But I knew it was wrong. I had to fight it. I had to have someone to keep me here."

His grip had lessened some. I stared at those fingers as if I could destroy them by sheer concentration.

"You, you don't understand at all. You've got family with you, she said you do. Doesn't matter if you're close or not." Rossi clearly wanted to back away from me as badly as he wanted to stay away from that passage behind him. He swayed within this tight perimeter. "This one here," his grip tightened briefly, "she wasn't wanted. Left out on the steps like an orphan. I knew I could convince her to come with me. We would be happy together. She'll see. And you didn't want her. You had your family."

"Is that what you want, Greta?" Had she really agreed to go with him?

Greta tried to shake her head, to disprove what Rossi was saying, but the hand that held her neck constricted her movements. I could see her answer, though, in her eyes. She might have agreed at the beginning, but she must have immediately seen how foolish such a decision had been.

"Rossi!" I said sharply, forcing him to look at me and to give up looking back over his shoulder, "she doesn't want to stay with you. Let her go."

"You don't need her. She doesn't need you." Desperation weighted his words.

Greta reached up, both hands now free, and gently took hold of the hand that held her throat. She began to pry the fingers loose.

"If I let her go," his voice faltered, "I'll have no choice."

His attention returned to the descending path behind him.

"Don't be stupid," I said. I'll admit my tone lacked compassion. "You're coming back up with us."

"No, I'm not." Rossi took a step back.

"Of course you are." Greta's voice filled the chamber for the first time. Both of us men stopped and looked at her. Greta reached out and took Rossi's hand.

"We'll stay together, the three of us."

I didn't like the sound of that.

"You will stay with me?" Rossi's face began to light up.

"No, I must stay with James. And you must stay in your own tomb. But that doesn't mean you'll be alone. Does it?"

A hollow reverberation, soaked with dread, rose out of the cavernous corridor below us. Rossi clamped his hand over Greta's and spun to face that sound. I took Greta's other hand and pulled her toward me.

"I won't be alone—" Rossi nearly whispered. I wasn't sure if it was a question or a declaration.

"No, you won't." Greta's soft tone filled the stone void. "We'll look after you."

"He won't let you," Rossi spoke as if in revelation. His eyes narrowed as he watched me with fear and hatred. "He'll keep you away. You know I'm right."

He might have been talking to her; he might have been talking to me. Either way we knew he was right. I knew my weakness. She knew it better.

It might have been that moment when I realized we were still holding her by her hands, one from each side, pulling steadily in opposing directions. We weren't hurting her, though her spirit was stretched beyond its natural shape. My fierce grip hurt her. His had to be doing the same. She no longer struggled against us, choosing instead to give in to both of us, her arms reaching out to each of us, as if she not only strained to save Rossi from descending to eternal damnation but also to reach back and save me from running away from my neighbor's desperate need.

She could not hold either of us close. Rossi neared the gate to the lower depths. I had almost reached the arch through which we could begin our ascent. Greta cried out as she realized she could not save both of us.

"Please, Jim! Dominic!" She would have to decide which one she most wanted to save. I wasn't going to let her. I couldn't allow her to bear the weight of that decision for all eternity. I was her husband, for

God's sake, and it was my responsibility to take the choice upon myself.

Using her as a point from which to pivot, I lunged forward, intent on breaking Rossi's hold on my wife. If he were determined to drop into the black levels below I would help him succeed. He would never get the chance to drag Greta this deep again. I would return her to the surface and she would never be lured down this path a second time.

We collided with all the anger, envy, fear, and resentment our spirits could project. It was enough. Crashing together with the force of two living brutes, our spirits grappling with our tangible natures, no longer holding on to Greta, we rolled through the black cavity and began our slide into the fourth circle of Hell.

A Night in the City of the Dead

(A Fanciful Tale)

"Good evening, Mayor."

"Good evening to you, kind sir."

"Good evening, Mayor."

"And to you, Ms. Leveaux."

The salutations were always the same. As the Mayor of New Orleans walked along the narrow streets of his realm, he tipped his hat first to one citizen then another. At every doorstep he passed, its occupant would look out with a kind word or at least call from within. It pleased the Mayor greatly to be treated so well and this was in fact his *raison d'etre* for his evening constitutional. Cynics accused him of merely trolling for votes, even in a non-election year, but the Mayor's close friends knew better. The Mayor simply adored being adored.

He was a short, big-boned figure; imposing in his tails and top hat. His high riding boots shone in the moonlight from innumerable polishings. His bold cheekbones and prominently white teeth shone just as bright. With a walking stick in his right hand, he clutched a cherry-red-tipped Hernsheim cigar between his fingers. The Mayor was proud of the fact that he had not gained an inch at his waist since—well, not since his death some sixty years in the past. But most importantly, he always said to intimates, he hadn't lost an ounce of his famous common sense, even without actually having a brain. A few of his former political rivals sniggered at this; they'd never thought he had any brains even when he was alive.

One street over from the Mayor, a smaller shorter skeleton, wearing nothing but a wool cap, rattled at full speed past tomb after tomb. Cutting sharply to his right, he caught sight of the Mayor and called out with a nervous voice—

"Mayah! Mistah Mayah, suh!"

"Two Penny Willie. My favorite little imp. What's all this about?"

"Ah'm glad Ah catched yah, Mayah." Two Penny stopped only a foot bone's length from the elected head of the City of the Dead and stood panting with his hands on his hipbones, trying like mad to draw air into the void that had once been his lungs. He had not run like that in ages.

"Deep breaths, lad." The Mayor put a steadying hand on the boy's shoulder. He was still holding the cigar and a few ashes dropped onto Two Penny's clavicle. The Mayor brushed at them absentmindedly. "What's this all about?"

"They's trouble—Ah don't like it—trouble's bad—" was all Two Penny managed to say.

An old woman's head peeked out from a crypt behind them in curiosity. She wore a cotton bonnet with a pair of spectacles perched on the bridge of her nose. The thick lenses only managed to highlight the empty cavities behind them.

"Is there trouble, Mayor?" she asked with more nosiness than fear.

"Do not fret, Widow Foche. I am trying to ascertain the facts at this very moment. Now Two Penny, please be specific."

"It's Captain Lahfeet—"

"Drunk again, no doubt," the Widow Foche interjected.

"Madam, if you please," the Mayor gently remonstrated.

"The Captain's threatenin' tah go ovah the wahll."

The Mayor pulled himself to full height. He jammed the cigar between his teeth and drew so hard on it the tip glowed with indignant fury. Blue smoke shot out around his jaw and the back of his skull.

"Have you informed the police?"

"Ah tried tah, Mayah. Sahgent Bones is—" Two Penny cast a quick look back at the inquisitive widow and leaned closer to the Mayor "—drunk, sah."

The Widow Foche huffed with a pleased disapproval.

"Two Penny, you've done well. Will you please tell my wife I'll be late for tonight's dinner party? She should still be in her chamber." He dug into his waistcoat pocket and pulled out two bright pennies. With a nod of approbation he dropped them into the lad's open hand. They clattered noisily as Two Penny closed his fingers over them and rattled his hands for good luck.

The Mayor carefully ground the tip of his cigar into the knob of his wrist, tucked it away inside a breast pocket of his jacket, and set off for the southeastern edge of the graveyard. St. Louis Cemetery Number One was enclosed by a solid wall of stone on all sides. The front gate stood in the middle of the eastern wall, a portion of which was six feet deep and filled with many citizens of that venerable city. This portion of the wall vaults rounded the southeastern corner and continued midway along that boundary.

"Going over the wall, is he?" the Mayor mumbled to himself. "We'll see about that."

"Just the man I'm looking for—" a short, fat-boned man with a white thatch of hair sticking out of the top of his skull stepped out from a large brick crypt.

"Not now, LeBoeuf. I cannot stop to talk."

"Then I'll walk with you," and LeBoeuf did just that. His spindly legs had to pump more often to keep up with the resolute strides of the Mayor. "You are indeed in a hurry."

"It's the Captain."

"Oh yes, I heard all about it. That Pirate!" LeBoeuf had to add a step every now and then to keep from falling behind. "He's the stubbornest scoundrel. Always has been. Has no right even to be in the city."

"Why were you looking for me?" The Mayor changed the subject. He did not want to speak about the Captain until he could hear the full story.

"It's Mother, she's taken to her crypt again and won't let anyone in."

"I'm sorry, old friend. But I keep telling you to treat her with more dignity. Times are changing. They don't put up with it like they did when we were young and masters of our world. Cato warned us two thousand years ago. 'Give women equality and they will be masters of us all' or something along those lines. If what we've been told is true, the men out there went and did the deed. There's no use fighting the consequences. And besides, I really don't think I can do anything. Your wife's demonstrations are hardly the business that should concern the Mayoral Offices."

"I think you're forgetting something."

"One moment," the Mayor put up a hand to interrupt. They had arrived at the western wall and approached a group of skeletons who stood facing a brazen fellow with a large three-cornered buccaneer hat cocked down over his brow. A much-faded crimson feather stuck crookedly out of a matching silk band.

"Aye, we'll be with ya," one of the grungier looking members of the mob stepped forward. "Do ye take us all?"

"No, my eager friend. I will only take two companions." Captain Jean Lafitte, the scourge of Barataria, stood casually in finely tailored grey breeches with a matching jacket and waistcoat. A white silk shirt could be seen just under his stiff cravat. A large steel sword was secured at his waist by a leather scabbard decorated with intricate gold and silver filigree. A strong bony hand rested on the cold, formidable hilt.

"You won't take anyone, Captain Lafitte." The Mayor stepped into the center of the gathering and faced the Pirate King. LeBoeuf stepped backwards into the shadow of a crypt and watched with trepidation.

"*Monsieur Le Maire*, I did not expect to be graced with your presence. I was expecting Sergeant Bones. This is, you understand, more his responsibility. I mean no offence."

"The Sergeant is attending to other matters," the Mayor said without hesitation. A few of the numbskulls behind him made exaggerated drunken movements and broke into rib tickling laughter. The Mayor ignored them and stuck out his chin as if such an action would remind them of his authority. "I was told you were contemplating an irregular sortie. Would you step aside with me for a private word?"

Lafitte nodded and held a hand out to one side. The Mayor passed through the crowd of impertinent urchins and led the Captain to one side of a large mausoleum whose stele had been worn down by the elements as to make the words impossible to discern.

"You mean to go over the wall, then?"

"That is my intention, M. Le Maire. Do you mean to stop me?"

"*I* do not need to stop you. The law is unbreakable and the fact of its existence will stop you." The Mayor did not doubt his own words in the least.

"May I remind you, respectfully of course, that I've been breaking the law since before you were born. I was, in fact, breaking the law under the very nose of your dearly departed father. A much stronger Mayor than you could have ever hoped to be."

"I'll not argue the point, Captain Lafitte. And no, you've no need to point out your lawlessness during my father's administration. He was telling us about your audacious behavior just the other night. To be frank, he still believes Col. Jackson acted completely irresponsibly in regards to your amnesty."

"In consideration of the fact that we are speaking in private and your slanderous statement goes no further than this, I'm prepared to ignore you and not demand retribution. But as a personal favor, I'd like to inform you that your father is not speaking the truth. He stood right inside the door of the Presbyter that night with Jackson and practically begged me to save his city. Really he was quite undignified in his reaction to the crisis. Whined a great deal. And when it was all over, he began to whine to the papers that Jackson and the Federal government had been too slow to act due to their prejudices regarding our French heritage. But I can assure you that it was *he* that failed to act as was his duty. His shifting of the blame was indefensible. That he was ever elected again was irresponsible."

"Be that as it may." The Mayor was not surprised to hear his father had been lying all these years, but he did not want to speak of it with Lafitte any further. "You have no legal recourse. The laws of the Dead City apply to all law abiding citizens; and apply to all lawbreakers as well."

"Then you have nothing to worry over. So why don't you go about your business?" Lafitte adjusted his cravat as if it were a signal of dismissal to the Mayor.

"Jean," the Mayor's voice softened as did his manner, "you've been law abiding for so many years now. What is this all about, eh?"

Lafitte pulled off his elaborate head covering and scratched the top of his skull with a well-manicured fingertip, the sound of which was much like a rat chewing on a coffin lid. He paused long enough to peer closely at this same fingertip to insure he had done it no damage. He said:

"I was told my old friend Dominique is not doing so well. I intend to see him."

"Jean, I am sorry to hear about M. You. He was always polite to me, and a great friend of the city. I will always respect what he did during the battle against the British, as well as his later work as a ward politician." The Mayor did not exaggerate his approbation. Dominique You was admired by many, despite having once been a trusted Lieutenant of Lafitte's. "But this talk of you going over the wall is batty. I beg of you, desist without further delay."

"*M. Le Maire*, you seem to have forgotten something of great import." Lafitte's gaze was arresting, even without eyes.

"And what is that?"

"Would you please point out which of these lovely tombs is my home?"

"Don't be absurd, Jean. I know you have no crypt."

"That is correct. I have no crypt, because I am not buried here." The Pirate Captain's face passed into shadow as he turned to examine the wall vault beside them. "You see many names here, but you will never find mine. I was buried far, far from this sacred ground. And yet here I am tonight."

"Yes, yes, I know all of this, Lafitte!" The Mayor's patience grew thin, as betrayed by his disrespect. "You have no city of your own, dumped in the sea so many years ago. And having wandered the floor of the Gulf many years, you found your way home and stole over the wall into our city, breaking more laws than I can bother to count."

"And how can I have done this? You said I must abide by the laws as every other citizen of this grave city." Lafitte lifted his chin and grinned hideously. "But you are very mistaken. I follow my own law, not the law as proscribed by neither the living nor the dead."

The Mayor, as affable a man as one could hope to be, felt his arms shake in anger, his finger bones curled into a fist. He knew the pirate was baiting him, trying to elicit a thrown punch or a contentious word. But the Mayor resisted the proffered bait, and kept a guard on his jawbone, as well as his fleshless fist.

"So that's it? You are above the law? What applies to us all does not apply to you?"

"Now, you are being absurd, sir. The laws apply to me as well as anyone. I simply choose to break them." Lafitte would have winked had he been able. "Don't look so exasperated, Mayor. You can rest assured I will face consequences. I have always known this, and been prepared to do so."

"Then stay," beseeched the Mayor, "M. You must already know of your concern, and undoubtedly finds comfort in the thought. It would needlessly distress him to discover you have borrowed trouble in order to visit him. Don't do this."

"I was never very good in dealing with men who said things like *don't do this*." He tossed his hat back on his skull as he quickly spoke. "I always felt the most urgent desire to do the exact opposite. Please, I pray thee, don't take this personally."

Digging a handful of fingers into a cracked portion of the wall vault just above his head, Lafitte stuck a boot onto a shelf from a vault on the second layer and jerked himself off the ground, grasping the mantel of the vault and swinging up and onto its crown. He perched atop the wall vault and cocked his head back in the Mayor's direction.

"Your hospitality has been above and beyond what I deserved, *M. La Maire*. I hope to be able to repay you in kind, one day. Though I cannot agree to your entreaty to stay, I will do you the honor of not taking any of your voters with me."

By this point, the crowd of onlookers had closed in, seeing the Pirate Captain on the wall. A wail of protest rose from their midst as they heard his intentions of leaving unescorted.

"Here, Captain, you promised!" A skeleton with baggy clothes, obviously once a very fat man, shook his arm at the elevated figure. His thin, bony arm stuck out crookedly from where the sleeve had fallen down to his shoulder. "Take ol' Charlie with you!"

"Captain Lafitte!" The call went up as they pressed closer, the foremost shoving hard against the Mayor.

"*Adieu, mon amis!*" Lafitte laughed deeply within his body, and leapt off the wall, into the black night beyond.

A gnashing of teeth signaled the horde's astonishment and anger at the Pirate Captain's desertion.

Many of the betrayed, recently certain they would be chosen to accompany Lafitte, turned their ire on the Mayor. One of the longest-boned men there stepped forward, interlacing his fingers and stretching them out until each bare knuckle popped as loud as pistol shots.

"Thet's yer fault, Gov'nah." He looked down upon the Mayor and sucked in a deep breath of air, all of which rushed right back out the top of his open and unclothed neck.

"Now, just one moment, sir." The Mayor stood as tall as he could, jutting out his white, sharp chin. "Remember who you are addressing. I am not the Governor. But I am the Mayor, and you will behave towards me with all due respect."

"Not lik'ly," the man growled through clenched teeth.

"Do you believe you are a lawbreaker in the vein of Captain Lafitte? I challenge you to consider this before you continue. Do not presume to be his equal. It will not go well for you."

Murmurs spread throughout the mass of the disturbed dead. A few of the more timid ones began to disappear into the twisted lanes of the city.

"What's this all about?" A rough voice boomed from behind the throng. A large man in uniform pushed through the startled mass. "Is there a problem here, Mr. Mayor?"

"Not at all," the Mayor kept his gaze on the tall malcontent. He briefly nodded at his chief law enforcer. "Sergeant Bones, these men and I were simply having a conversation. We were all gravely disappointed to learn that Captain Lafitte has gone over the wall. A shocking breech of the law."

"Over the wall?" Sergeant Bones scraped his jaw with a set of knuckles. "Once a Pirate, always, eh?"

"Yes, to be sure. You should have been watching him. In future, you will temper your drinking, Sergeant." The Mayor's voice was soft. His words were a matter of duty, not anger.

"Over the wall?" Sergeant Bones asked again. He scraped his jaw again. A slight bristle coat of whiskers forever hampered his attempts to appear clean and orderly. It was a great embarrassment to the officer of the law. "I can't say I'm sorry he's gone, Mr. Mayor. That's one I'm glad to be rid of."

"An attitude that many will take, I am sure. Nonetheless, Sergeant, it should never have happened. Now if you will excuse me, I have a Dinner Party for which I am late. Good night, good peoples of the city. I bid you return to your family homes in an orderly manner. See to it, Sergeant."

"At once," snapped Sergeant Bones. Raising his voice, he turned upon those still crowding the narrow lane. "You heard the Mayor. Move your tired sack of bones out of here. Don't make me crack yer skulls!"

The horde of rickety frames clattered in a rush to get as far from the Sergeant's reach as possible.

Come Out, My Love

The first night he came to her crypt, he was drunk. He was stinking drunk. He stood in front of her white stone tomb leaning heavily to one side. From his point of view the cemetery was tilted—everything was tilted, except her. The freshly chiseled marble faceplate sat squarely in the center of the world and everything else radiated away from her at bent angles. That was how he viewed it. He kept thinking of the crypt as *her*. He vaguely understood it was only her dried out body that was inside it, but the alcohol kept confusing him. The crypt transformed into a white marble woman. He reached out to her. She was cold. *Hard.* He pressed his hand against her as if he could break her outer shell and reveal her warmth and love buried within. He tried to smash it.

He broke two knuckles and vomited into her marble flower vase.

It was the first and last time Peter Young climbed the wall of Saint Louis Cemetery Number Two drunk.

"This is better than my last gift, Diana." Peter gently placed seven white roses into the marble vase and tried to arrange them into something symmetrical. One of the roses refused to stand up and Peter kept leaning it against the other roses. "I'm afraid to even ask your forgiveness about the other night. I can't explain—no, that's not right. I don't know how to explain what was going on."

He knew how to explain why he had been drunk. He just did not want to tell her the truth.

"Seven white roses, honey. See? One for each year. I know, you don't have to say it. It's not our anniversary. But I just thought it would be nice. I remember how you loved the white roses you saw that day we went up to the Evangeline Oak. What was that, four years ago? You remember? We had Carl's car. You said 'I could get used to a German car' and I asked if you could get used to living in poverty."

A tour guide led four people down the row of tombs and passed within an arm's length of where Peter stood. He allowed his mind to drift back to that day and closed his eyes.

"We don't need a car anyway," Diana said dismissively.

"Yeah, I guess." Peter knew she was trying to make him feel better. She never let him dwell on his lack of financial success. "You hungry? I'm gonna pull in here."

She pulled cotton flats over her bare feet and pulled down the cover on the vanity mirror.

"Don't even say it," Peter preempted her, "you do not look like a mess. You're as pretty as those flowers. Look, do you like those? They're white roses."

It was a pastime of theirs. Peter was always on the lookout for flowers that she liked. Her tastes were narrow and it had become a joke between them. She especially seemed to hate any flowers he suggested.

"Oh, damn it." Peter's eyes flew open and he stared at the seven roses.

"I can't stand white roses."

He could still hear her voice after four years. How could he have forgotten? He reached down and snatched the roses from her vase.

"I'm sorry, my love. I don't know what I was thinking." He tossed the roses between two crypts that stood opposite Diana's. "As usual, I'm spending all my time apologizing to you. You must get tired of that. Don't worry about the roses. I'll bring some red ones. You do like the red ones, don't you?"

He stood staring at the silent crypt as if expecting an answer. A wasp drifted near him but he ignored it. He stared at the sealed edge of her marble faceplate. The mistake with the roses had set him on edge. He wiped his sleeve across his forehead and drew in a long breath.

"Diana, I'll tell you why I was drunk." Peter swallowed to keep his voice from cracking. "You won't like this. I took Melinda Carter out for dinner. I'm getting lonely. I finally got the courage to—"

He could not finish the sentence. A beetle crawled into view on one of the steps of Diana's crypt. Peter allowed himself to be distracted. The fat, black bug marched at a steady pace and crawled over the rotted shell of a lizard. The late morning sun shone brilliantly on the beetle's blue-black folded wings. He had to say it. Peter could never explain to anyone. But he knew he had to say it. He had to make her understand.

"—the courage to replace you." His hands trembled as he spoke. He steadied them by grasping his wedding band and polishing it with his thumb. "Don't be angry. Don't go away. Let me explain it all. You'll understand when I finish. Diana?"

The beetle was still marching. It had passed into shadow but had seemed not to notice. Far off to the left Peter could hardly hear the steady drone of the tour guide's voice washed out by the hum of passing cars on the raised section of Interstate 10 that created the shadow.

"I was only kidding myself. I knew that as soon as we sat down to dinner. You remember Melinda, don't you? She's no Hollywood beauty, but she's attractive and smart; talking with her is easy, delightful. But I knew right away none of that mattered. It was empty. I realized I wouldn't have cared if she were ugly, stupid— she could have sat there the whole night talking about anything. Even if she'd been rich it wouldn't have mattered. It wasn't you. I knew I couldn't do it. I couldn't be without you."

The white crypt stood silently as a gentle breeze danced among the neighboring tombs.

"I got drunk because I knew there was only one thing to do. I knew I could not live—didn't want to live anymore. And so I tried to drink enough to forget that I had decided to end my own life. There wasn't enough. I couldn't forget. After I left here, I sat on the stoop, back at our place, and I couldn't stop thinking about it. The pain I felt was worse than the pain in my hand. See this here? I broke two knuckles that night. I know, I'm an idiot. But my heart was hurting worse than that. I couldn't see any way around it. I really had decided to kill myself. Until *it* occurred to me."

Peter stepped close to Diana's grave, afraid to be overheard. He brushed his bangs from his eyes in an effort to calm his nervousness. She had to understand, he told himself. *She must!*

"It was almost so simple I nearly missed it. But there it was, as clear as day. I realized there was no reason I had to die. Because there was another option. You could come back to me!"

His fingertips barely touched her crypt's roofline. He stroked it, not sure if he did so as one lover stroking another lover's bare hip or as a desperate man rubbing the rounded sides of a golden lamp.

"You don't know how much I need you. Don't laugh at me. I'm not joking with you. Our love was pure. You know that! That's why you can come back to me. Come back! Come out!"

His sobs forced him to stop talking and he dropped to his knees, startling the beetle. The sun warmed his exposed neck. He twisted his head and tried looking directly into it. *The sun!* Why hadn't he thought of it before? He stumbled back to his feet.

"I understand, darling. The sun. It's the sun, right? This isn't the time. I'll come back. Wait for me! Prepare yourself, my love."

Peter left Diana's tomb. The beetle had gone as well. The sun disappeared behind a cloud and only her whitewashed crypt stood unmoved. The marble plate remained sealed. Diana's decayed form lay immovable in the grave.

He had rehearsed his words over and over again. But in the end, he had only been able to utter the one thought that dominated him.

"I need you! Come out to me, Diana! *I need you!*"

The sun was gone, and the darkness was nearly complete. The cold night carried no moon. Peter stood in front of the crypt with his shoulders and spirits hanging in despair. His cry did not echo off the stone blocks surrounding him. His cry was too feeble for that; a dry, raspy whisper.

"I need you!"

But what did it mean, he asked himself. What nobility was there in needing someone? What significance did that carry? Surely not enough to break the laws of nature. There had to be more. Diana had always taught him to think like that. But of course there was more to his desire for her than need. He needed her and she had always needed him. There was a basic, natural order that had been bigger than both of them. They had even joked about it. It worked both ways with them: a symbiotic relationship. They had learned to accept it early on.

But did that matter? What nobility was there even in being needed? If a need were so visceral as to exclude personal choice, could there exist any virtue in the expression of that need? And what higher good came from needing or being needed? To what could he appeal in Diana's spirit? *You're needed, come back!* As if that changed everything?

It changed nothing. Peter knew it. Her crypt remained sealed, holding her in. He had to find another way. Needing her made no difference in the world; need meant nothing.

But she had meant everything to him. Without her there had been no meaning to life. Peter felt a tug in the depths of his mind. Surely that was the secret of their love. They had fit together like two factors in a complex equation, an equation that was senseless without them. A rush of blood to his head filled him with a clarity he had never expected. The words came forth without hesitation:

"Diana! You mean everything to me. Without you there *is* no meaning. Come out!" He sank to his knees and watched the crypt expectantly. The night wind stirred, a few large trucks rumbled above him on the interstate, but Diana remained locked in stone.

"You still mean the world to me," Peter could barely utter the words, but he did speak them loud enough to hear them. *The world?* He thought. He reluctantly examined his own boast. Had she indeed meant everything to him? She'd been light where he had previously known darkness. Joy to his sorrow. These were simple truths that were easy to say and impossible to prove. And *that* was something Diana would have said. Maybe she was saying it now with her stony silence.

Then what was it? Peter silently demanded. He'd always asked her such questions in silence, afraid to show his anger when she had been alive. He knew he was still afraid to question her, even as she lay in her shell of death. *Just what is it that will make you listen?*

"An apology?" Peter muttered. He lifted his head and his gaze tried to pierce through the marble. "Do I have to crawl? Do you want tears? Is that all I have to say? *I'm sorry? I didn't know you were hurting?"* How could he have known? She'd hid it until the end. She'd hid it all until she chose to end it. "How could I have known you were in such despair? I'm sorry I didn't see it! *Why didn't you tell me? How could you leave me?"*

The last questions hung in the darkness like the wail of a dying spirit. Peter trembled as he realized what he'd said. For the first time that night, he watched the seal on her crypt with trepidation. What if Diana really did come out? Fear crept into his heart, and Peter wavered in his desire for her return.

"No, I'm not blaming you." He tried to correct his mistake. He would not allow his pettiness to rise up and interfere with his plans. It had been that very nature that had driven her to despair when she'd been alive. He searched for words that might undo the damage. "My love, I'm only tired. And hurting—hurting for your love. It might not matter that I need you. I may not be able to prove you mean the world to me. And it's no matter if I say I'm sorry or you say you forgive me. Those words don't have to be said. What really matters is *I love you.*"

Too many words were rushing through his head now. He was not sure which words had been said out loud and which ones had only been whispered. Was she angry with him now? Had he shown her too much anger? Did she know he despised her for her choice? What did she know? What had she known before she'd died? What had really pushed her to take her own life? He tried in vain to free his mind from the paralysis of his fears.

"I love you, Diana. That's all that matters. Come out! Come out!"

Her crypt stood as silent as every tomb in that burial ground. In the moonless dark, Peter could only stare at her shapeless house of the dead with tears rolling down his cheeks. He waited for her to stir. *Come out. Come out.*

"So you love me, will that change everything?" Was that her voice? Peter wanted it to be. "Did I ever ask for your love? Did your love chain me and enslave me to you? Does your love give you power over me? Must I come when beckoned? Will I stay if you demand it?"

Peter tried to ignore the voice, deciding it had only come from within himself. And while it might have been something she would have said, he would not believe they were actually her words.

"Was I obligated to return your love?" it asked.

Come out, just come out. This doesn't matter.

Peter leaned against the inscribed marble, his mind rejecting the words he had heard. It could not have been her. He knew that. It had been his own thoughts the voice had spoken. Thoughts he had buried along with the body of his wife. Thoughts he had buried and replaced with every good memory he had been able to dig up. Good memories that had convinced him with an overpowering certainty that she must come back; that she would come out when called.

He stayed there at her crypt for another hour. He wanted to believe he was still waiting for the seal to break; for Diana to answer his call. He would not believe he was watching to ensure she stayed safely confined behind the marble. What he feared to believe was that it mattered little what he did. She had made her choice long ago, and he had never had any power over her. He had needed her, he had found meaning with her, and he had loved her.

Inside the chamber, Diana's remains lay in total darkness. Her hands, or what was left of them, were no longer crossed on her bosom. As skin had shriveled in the heat, and her flesh had wasted away, her arms had unfolded as if pulled apart by the grim reaper to make her all the more vulnerable to his ancient art. Her jaw had collapsed in much the same way, the tattered remains of her mouth forming a shape suggesting imminent speech. The muffled words of her husband haunted the darkness of the crypt.

Come out.

Diana did not move. She said nothing. Fingers traced the seal of the marble slab, searching for a chink; a way to break the seal. There were none. Peter continued to trace the outline, unable to recall how it felt to stroke his lover's flesh, and unsure if he really wanted to remember.

Mugging the Dead

"Don't run off like that, darlin'!" The man's voice was sharp. A little rough.

"Ah right," the woman's reply was soft, almost impossible to hear. She added in an even softer voice— "Ah didn't *run* off."

"Oh now, don't act like that." Some of the harshness left his voice, replaced with gentle exasperation. "I'm tryin' to look after ya. You remember what I read out loud back at the hotel, huh? We gotta watch out for muggers in this place. Says right there, see?"

A sound of paper being rattled and shaken followed his insistent tone.

"Now come on, we gotta stay up with the group."

"Let's don't, Chester." The woman used her accent to draw sympathy from the man—*Ches-tah*. "Maybe they only say it to make yah think yah gotta take the tour. Let's walk awhile by ourselves. It's so quiet, and pretty."

"Darlin', this ain't like your little hometown. We're in the *big* city, now. And these here funny graveyards are dangerous. They got muggers hiding out behind these overgrown tombstones. They ain't makin' that up. And say what you like, it's just a graveyard. Ain't nuthin' pretty 'bout it."

The woman spoke softly again in reply. This time she spoke too softly to be heard. But the tone was unmistakably submissive. Chester continued to defend his point as they moved along the row of crypts and hurried to catch up to their group.

"I wish you'd listened to Darlin', *Ches-tah*."

A short man wearing blue jeans and a solid blue t-shirt stepped out from behind a heavily deteriorated crypt and stared down the grassy row. He was clean-shaven, with hair cropped close to his scalp. He was holding a baseball cap in one hand, and a small knife in the other.

"Damn brochures. Who reads those, anyway? How's a mugger supposed to make a living with bad publicity like that?" Folding the knife and slipping it into a back pocket, the mugger walked off down a row perpendicular to the one taken by the tourists. Smashing the hat on his head, he walked through the cemetery without the slightest interest in the historic artifacts that surrounded him.

His name was Eddie Williams. He was forty-three years old, and looked more like he was ten or fifteen years older. He had spent many years working shrimp boats out of Morgan City, and just as many roustabouting on the platforms in the Gulf. After three failed marriages and even more failed jobs, he was employed full time as a mugger. It's a title he used when thinking of himself. It didn't bother him, he had no more scruples about that. He would have argued that he was no thief, no pickpocket, no smash-and-grab artist. But that was only for accuracy's sake. A mugger was separate from those others only by definition. He had no delusions that one was any better than the other. He was simply a mugger; no more, no less.

Disappointed that the tourists had given up the idea of sightseeing alone, Eddie sought out a quiet secluded corner of the cemetery and lay down in the shade of a large family crypt. It was early afternoon, and the sun was still high. A front had rolled in the night before from the north, pushing the humidity off the city, if only temporarily. In the shade, the air was comfortable. It nearly felt like fall had arrived. Eddie lay on his back, and covered his eyes with an arm. He fell asleep without the slightest hesitation. The Cities of the Dead carried no mystery or dread with him. He had abandoned mysteries at the end of his third marriage.

The door of the confessional snapped shut; after that, only silence.

"Are you there, child?" The priest finally asked.

"Hello, Jack."

"That's a little different. No more 'bless me Father for I have sinned'?" The priest had recognized the voice of his boyhood friend and at the same time recognized the gravity of his tone. His attempt at levity fell flat.

"No, no more of that."

"So why are you here, Eddie?" The voice came through the screen with only a hint of condemnation.

"As an old friend, I wanted to tell you. I wanted to be honest with you."

"So you've made your decision? You're giving up your faith?"

"Yeah, from your point of view, I guess. But not mine. Kids don't give up believing in Santa. You tell them the truth, and after that—there's no Santa. It's no longer a matter of believing. And it's not a matter of giving up that belief. Belief is no longer viable."

"And what will you believe in now, Eddie?"

"That's the same kind of thinking, Jack. As if I have to believe in something else. But you know, kids don't have a gaping void to fill once they find out Santa's make-believe. All they usually come away with is disappointment—learn to distrust a little more."

"You have done me the honor of coming here and telling me your decision," the priest hesitated and then said "follow me."

He left the confessional, not looking back to see if he had been heeded. With a strong stride, he moved into the nave down the row of pews towards the chancel. Just to the right of the chancel railings, he opened a small door and disappeared. Eddie had followed out of curiosity and was only a step behind him. The small door sealed shut. They were in a small Chantry Chapel.

"So what is this?" Eddie looked around the closet-sized chapel.

"This is where I do you the honor of telling you what I have to say." The priest's voice was no longer gentle and fatherly. He was using a voice he had not used in a very long time. He stuck a finger in Eddie's chest and leaned into him.

"You feel sorry for yourself. Your third wife has left you, and all you can do is blame God for it. You lost another job. You were fired, to be more specific. Fired for failing another drug test. You can't give up that damned weed, and everything has fallen apart because of it. Who do you blame? You? Heaven forbid, right? But then, I guess you don't believe in heaven anymore. You can't even blame God anymore since you've dropped him from your reality as well. You're being stupid, Eddie. Your life is already shot to hell. And now you're going to go it alone? You're going to throw God out of the boat?"

"That's fine words for a priest."

"A little profane for you? You'd better get used to it. You can't imagine the implications of stepping out from under His protection."

"Look at me, Jack. I've never been under protection. And if I have, it's protection I can do without."

Eddie looked into a black sky. A wind blew the heavy leaves of magnolia trees. He heard footsteps—

some running, some only walking. He watched the swaying shadows of the trees and decided he was only hearing the leaves. Clarity returned to his mind; he had been asleep. A deep and long sleep. The moon was well on its way to its zenith in the black night.

Eddie stood and brushed dried bits of leaves and grass from his back. He was not concerned to be in the middle of the cemetery at night. It wasn't his first time. He had long ago discarded childish superstitions. He had, in fact, cast off all forms of imagination. To him, the only difference darkness brought to the cemetery was the absence of tourists.

It was, therefore, much to his surprise when he saw movement out of the corner of his eye. To his right, he spied a figure walking past a crypt that was large enough to hold sixteen caskets. Eddie backed between two crypts and reached into his pocket for his knife. The figure came close enough to be seen by the moonlight. He was taller than Eddie by at least half a foot. He was slender, with an exceedingly well-groomed mustache. Although Eddie did recognize the man's clothing was nearly straight out of a Charles Dickens novel, he did not stop to consider this. Without stopping to consider anything, Eddie boldly stepped out into the open and put the knife to the man's throat.

"Kind of late for a stroll. Haven't you heard this is a dangerous place?"

"Excuse me?" The man stared at his assailant with well-bred arrogance.

"This won't take long, old man. Just carefully hand over any money you're carrying." Eddie backed off a step, allowing the man room to reach for his wallet.

"Is this a joke? I don't carry money."

Eddie closed the distance to his victim and put the point against the man's fleshy neck. "No joke. What's that on your hand?"

"What does it look like? It's a ring."

"Take it off. Come on, give it to me. And that—" Eddie poked his knife at the man's waistcoat. He tapped the hard gold shell of a pocket watch.

"Now see here," the man began to protest. Eddie reached out quickly and struck the man on his chin. The older man fell back against a crypt wall. He ran his hand over his jaw as if to make sure it was still where it should be. "You have no idea who I am."

"You have no idea how little I care."

"I'm beginning to get one." The man deftly removed his ring and pocket watch. He held them out to Eddie with cold indifference.

"That could have been painless, but I don't care either way." Eddie snatched at the valuables and backed away. He ran off into the semidarkness of the moonlit night. Stepping up onto a low coping tomb, he scrambled up onto a higher crypt. From there, he stepped from tomb to tomb, never touching the ground. In this way he quickly covered the length of the graveyard. With a little effort he jumped from the last crypt onto the solid perimeter crypt wall. He paused to catch his breath, listening for signs of pursuit.

No alarm had been raised. No hue and cry for help. He could hear no clattering of footsteps. The old man had evidently accepted his fate. Eddie was not surprised. People were like that. They were quick to give in to the evil that befell them, as if they shared some common guilt that demanded payment in the form of oppression. Eddie didn't care what made people act like that. He was only glad they *did* act like that.

Watching carefully along the quiet street, he prepared to jump down on the outside of the crypt wall. He was not sure just how late it was, but it appeared to be late enough that there was no traffic on the street. Eddie swung his legs over the edge then stopped. He was very certain he had just heard someone crying.

Turning one ear back in the direction of the crypts behind him, he held still, then held his breath. He heard it again. There was, in fact, a woman crying. The distinction was easy to make; a soft whimpering played off the crypts in the flow and ebb of the night wind.

Who in the hell is that? Eddie swung back around and dropped quietly onto the grass. He had never encountered anyone in the cemetery after the gates were closed. And yet, not only had he found someone to mug, there was now a second opportunity. Staying in shadows as much as possible, he followed the sound of the woman. She was on the second row to his left. He leaned around the corner of a crumbling monument to the Krupp family and saw her only ten yards beyond.

A young woman knelt before a well-cared-for tomb. She was dressed in a white gown. Her golden hair was tied into a bun low on the back of her head. She held a bouquet of melancholy flowers in her arms. As Eddie watched, she bent forward and set them with loving care on a chipped marble shelf that extended from the right side of the crypt's stele.

Eddie was in no way touched by the scene. He saw immediately that she was vulnerable in her mourning. It would require very little effort to do the job. He boldly walked around the corner of the Krupp tomb and approached her. She did not see him coming. With her eyes fastened on the flowers, and clouded by tears, he startled her as he spoke.

"I hope you don't mind if I interrupt."

She turned towards him in confusion. "Pardon me, sir?"

"I like that very much." Eddie's eyes fixed on the sparkling necklace that lay upon her milky white neck. The silver chain and jeweled settings reflected moonlight with dazzling intensity. "Give me your necklace. And don't fool around. I don't want to hurt you."

"My—" her hand felt for the thing and her confusion grew. "You cannot mean you are a thief."

"I'm not a thief. You're being mugged. You can call me a robber, but either way, you're going to give me the necklace." He brought the knife up to make sure she could see it clearly.

The woman pulled back swiftly from him with speed he never thought she could possess. She stood now, though the long gossamer gown covered her so completely she might have looked as if she were floating just above the threshold of the crypt to a man with an imaginative mind. But Eddie had no such thing. He stood his ground, angry that yet another victim dared to resist.

"The necklace, you bitch!" Eddie crowded her against the tomb. He grabbed for the necklace but her cold hand blocked him. Her mournful eyes transformed into fiery light as she fought him off. By this time, any observer would have plainly seen that the gown was a full six inches off the threshold. But Eddie's eyes were fixed only on the jewels.

"Who has known such boldness?" The woman's voice was no longer soft. She spoke with rising fury. "You dare to violate me upon this sacred ground?"

The night wind had increased with the force of her words. Leaves swirled around Eddie and his victim. In fighting for the necklace, her hand had clamped down on his. Eddie was surprised at her strength, but more so at her courage and anger. She was hissing, her fingers digging into his wrist. With blunt force he threw her against the crypt. A shriek escaped her open mouth as her coal red eyes seethed with rage.

"You shall never possess it." She rasped with an otherworldly resonance. "You tread the path of everlasting death in your lust and sacrilege. Yours will be torment and death!"

"Not at your hands, lady." Eddie wrenched his wrist free of her grasp and backhanded her across her cheek. She fell into the grass, her head coming to rest on the marble threshold. Her hair had fallen loose from its bun and lay spread like debris from a storm. Eddie ripped the necklace from her throat.

"No," she whispered, unable to rise or even lift her head. "Not by my hand."

"Crazy lady," Eddie muttered; rubbing his wrist, trying to regain circulation. As he walked away, he could hear her cry feebly for help.

Violence was nothing new to Eddie. He had found it necessary to make good on his threats every once in a while in the pursuit of his profession. But he had never seen a woman act like such a hellion. Once a woman was cornered on her own, she was most likely to submit in fear for her life, if not more importantly her virtue. It was an advantage he always pressed. But he never found pleasure in the act of violence. And he was angry he had been forced to commit it.

He held the necklace up in the moonlight and inspected it. Judging by the woman's irrational efforts to protect it, he decided that it must not only be valuable. There had to be sentimental value in it. He shrugged at the thought. For him, there was no profit in sentiment.

Historical value could be turned into cash. But not sentiment.

The woman's pleas were still audible.

Standing at the crypt wall again, he briefly wondered at the presence of two individuals inside the cemetery after the gates had been closed. Maybe they had been left open? He considered the possibility. He glanced down the open row in the darkness towards the gates. He could not see them clearly even with the aid of the moon. Large and ancient oaks stood guard outside the gates and shrouded them in thick shadows. Eddie began to wonder just how possible it was they might be open.

Approaching the gates on that wall, he almost had to touch them before he could clearly see that the black iron was locked shut. He wrapped his fingers around one of the bars and jerked at it. The gates held steady. Eddie circled the full perimeter and found each of the four sets of gates secured as they always were each night.

He could no longer hear the woman. Had she been able to scale the walls? She was surely too small to do so, most certainly too weak. Still angry at being pushed to violence, he headed back in her direction. Had she passed out? He did not want her to die. It would lead to a great outcry and the police would be out in full force. It would ruin his workplace. Force him to relocate. The thought angered him even more.

He rounded the corner at the Krupp tomb and stopped dead in his tracks. The woman was gone. In her place stood a man in a long, black coat. Shadows hid his face.

"Where did you come from?" Eddie was beginning to think the cemetery had become a train station.

"I was summoned." The newcomer's smile was just visible in the darkness.

"What are you, the police?" Eddie made ready to dash back around the Krupp memorial if the man made one aggressive move towards him.

"You're a very dull man, Edward Williams. To be plain—you're very stupid."

"I had a priest who called me that once." At the mention of the priest the man in black twitched. Eddie ignored this and continued to speak. "But he may have been more stupid than me. You might be just as stupid. Haven't you heard these graveyards are no place to wander around? You never know what dangerous types you might run into."

Eddie casually put his hand in his pocket. Although the man was much bigger than Eddie, he was not afraid of him. However, he felt instinctively that if a fight could be avoided it should be. The man stood too confidently. Eddie had often measured his victims by their confidence. But it was never the sole factor in his equation.

"You're right. You never know what you'll run into here." A chill wind blew down the row of tombs each time the man in black spoke.

"So it's a big secret who you are. Well, who summoned you? That crazy woman?"

"She did," the man nodded slowly, "among others. You have had a growing reputation. But tonight you have finally crossed over to the other side."

"And what side is that?" Eddie eased the knife from his pocket. He had no earthly interest in what the man was saying. He was simply playing for time.

"My side." Sulfurous breath accompanied his words.

"I had no intention of hurting her." Eddie ignored the poisonous odor and concentrated on the man. He was ten, maybe twelve yards away. He studied the black figure, looking for weakness. There was none. His stance was solid, his arms hung loosely at his side.

He did not fidget from one foot to the other. He stood firm with purpose.

"That does not matter anymore. What matters is that I am here for you."

Sulfur poured forth from the figure now, falling about them like a mist. A low growl sounded in the lower tones of his voice.

Eddie tightened his fingers over the handle of his knife. It was evident the man was a lunatic. What could make him so bold? If he was not with the police, what could he possibly want? Eddie thought he just might know what it was.

"You're out of your mind. Do you think you can come in here and take these from me?" Eddie dug into his pocket with his free hand and held the pocket watch and necklace up together. "Do you think I'm so old and weak that I'd roll over and let you take my place?"

The moonlight broke from behind a cloud and illuminated the black figure's face. Eyes of a swirling red and yellow smoldered in deep sockets. A sharp snarl escaped his cruel lips and his teeth snapped. Jerking one hand up, he closed his fist over the necklace and gold watch, which had flown at him as if shot from a cannon.

"These baubles?" A low laugh. "Useless." With a flick of his wrist he cast them into the air. They rose only a few feet before stopping in mid-air—suspended and twinkling in the moonlight.

Eddie grew enraged at the sight of his plunder taken from him. He trembled as he held himself in check. Not yet. Not yet.

"Thief! Pickpocket! You've no right!" Eddie slid the blade from its casing with a snap of his thumb. "No right at all!"

"Like I said at the beginning. You're a stupid man, Edward Williams. You're exactly the kind of man I want."

"Fool!" Eddie rocked back on his heels and drew energy from his rage. "It doesn't matter if you want me. Because you're going to have more of me than you can handle."

Eddie spit contemptuously on the tomb beside him. The dark figure lowered his head into shadow. Only the eyes could still be seen, glowing with desire.

Eddie charged across the open space between them into the shadow that streaked toward him like a great black bird of prey.

Grave Robber

He rolled it around in his hand watching the glint of moonlight off its facets. It would be worth a good bit of money. There was some satisfaction in that, but not as much as he used to feel. With a subconscious need to increase his risk, a desire to feel some adrenaline, he switched on his flashlight and passed its beam over the object he now held between two fingers. The opal ring sparkled in the darkness. His heartbeat picked up in rhythm as he admired the fire in the center of the pale stone. It was set with six diamonds attending it, forming a ring of brilliant stars. He switched off the light.

In the deeper darkness that followed the light, Martin sat motionless, waiting for his eyes to readjust to the void around him. He looked to his left down the row of tombs; their squat temple-like shapes disappearing after only a dozen yards. He turned and peered into the opened crypt before him, and saw only a heavy shadow outlined in a lighter shade of shadow. He could just make out the cover of the grave leaning against the adjoining tomb. He decided he was done. There was nothing left of the old woman's eternal accoutrements worth removing. With great effort, and wishing now his old partner still worked with him, he wrestled the cover back onto the above ground burial chamber. Once it was safely balanced and could be held with one hand, he shone the light inside the grave one last time, in case he'd missed anything of value.

Martin felt unexpectedly conscious of the corpse that lay before him. He had never paid attention to the bodies before; but this one held his attention. He ran the light up over the loose and heavy dress until it rested on the woman's face. The skin was like tightly wrapped leather, the face sunken, as if it were the face of a rag doll that had long ago lost its stuffing. The framework of bone was sharply visible under this. Martin killed the light and forced the cover back into place.

He gathered his tools and spoils and escaped the cemetery.

Martin Broder sold automobiles. His grave robbing was only a sideline. In the golden light of day, he stood on the showroom floor and anxiously descended on customers who pushed open the glass doors with wide-eyed desire. Rubbing his long fingered, bony hands in anticipation, he smiled broadly and preached with passion on the virtues of the latest models. From his towering height of six feet and six inches, he could command an audience with awe as he demonstrated the wonders of vehicular manufacturing.

But no prospective clients darkened the door that morning. He slowly walked the length of the showroom thinking of the ring he'd found in the old woman's grave. To his surprise, he could not visualize the ring. Instead, the woman's face dominated his memory. With curiosity he perused the image. He felt no revulsion; no fear of her death mask. Much to the contrary, he was fascinated by what he had seen. Never had he paid such close attention to a corpse. The woman had not been very old—maybe close to sixty. It was nearly impossible to tell in her present condition. He had only known her age by the marble inscription. But he convinced himself that she had been beautiful, if only in a common way. The face was peaceful though certainly a little weary.

Why had he never noticed the faces of the other corpses, he wondered? What had they been like? Had any of them looked as peaceful? Had there been any that had deteriorated beyond recognition? Or had some of them looked exactly like they had the day death had come to their door? Martin sought in vain for any memory from his countless forays into the Cities of the Dead. It shocked him to realize he had no recollection of any other faces save the old woman with the opal ring. Had he subconsciously hid his eyes from the faces of the dead?

He pondered this mystery over dinner that night, to the point that his wife interrupted his silence.

"Are you sick? A headache?"

"No," he answered her. He said nothing more. And she, a stout red-faced woman with very little interest in her husband, was satisfied with his answer. She had done her duty; fed him, and made sure he was not ill. She retreated to the kitchen, leaving him alone.

He was not sick. To the contrary; he was alive with an excitement he had not felt for many years. He was intrigued. There rose within him a blooming sensation of—he was startled to put it into words—*desire*. He wanted to see not just the old woman again, but he wanted to see the others; those dead souls from whom he had previously robbed. What had *they* looked like?

The thought had become unbearable. He had not planned to make a raid that night. His hard and fast rule had always been never twice in one week. That was tempting fate. He consoled himself with the realization that this was really not a raid. He wasn't planning to take anything. All he really wanted to do was look. That would be all right.

He knew just where he would start; the old man who had been buried with the diamond studded walking stick. That had brought him a very nice paycheck. Martin felt a rush of blood that left his head spinning. There would be no more arguments. He knew he had to see the dead man's face that very night. Nervously, he left the table and rushed out towards the back door.

"Where are you off to?" his wife tried to block his exit.

"Out." Martin spoke with rare boldness. He pushed past her.

"Now what's fired him up?" Mrs. Broder stuck her hands on her hips and watched him dash across the back yard. "He's not acted like that since he was a young buck on the trail of my scent."

She had ceased to see her man as anything approaching a young buck and so did not worry over his peculiar agitation any more that night.

Martin made his way over the crypt wall that ran around Lafayette Cemetery Number One with greater agility than he ever had in the past. He headed straight for the old man's crypt and found it with ease. The ornate, church shaped crypt had an unusually tall spire and a solemn, sword-wielding angel stood guard beside its entrance. Martin was pleased to see the angel still in its place. He despised those thieves who would steal the statuary outside the crypts. Yes, they were valuable, but such desecration of the beauty of the cemetery was reprehensible to him. Removing jewelry and other valuables from inside the crypts was forgivable, he had always reasoned; the sanctity of the site *appeared* unmolested. To Martin, there was a world of difference between the two.

So intent was he on seeing the old man's face that he hardly noticed the new and improved lock on the crypt door. With only a flicker of an amused grin at the elaborate hardware, he worked the lock open faster than usual. Scraping open the heavy door, he ducked into the crypt and shined his light.

He uttered a cry of dismay. Despair drained him of energy as he stared at the coffin sitting on the stand. It was new. The flowers, though dead, looked only a few months old. He should have known. The old man had been removed after desiccation had reduced him to dust and another family member required the space. Martin, flush from his eagerness to see the man's face, tried to breathe in the dark confines of the tomb.

"And so," Martin whispered softly, "who are *you*?"

His disappointment vanished with the question. Who was it, indeed? He knew right then he had to look. A dozen questions bombarded him in that brief moment; was it a man or woman? Old? Ugly or beautiful? His hands trembled as he fumbled with the latches on the casket. As he raised the lid, he took a breath and looked upon the face.

It was the face of a dead girl. She could not have lived more than twenty years upon this earth. A small pixie nose sat between widely spaced eyes and small, pursed lips. Martin felt a gentle disappointment in the fact that she was not beautiful. But that shallow thought passed as he gazed at her pale, plastic features and thought how lifeless and unreal she looked. He understood that beauty meant nothing to this cadaver anymore. If she had ever fretted over her plain demeanor, she certainly no longer gave it any thought. Had she ever been kissed by anyone other than her parents? It was most likely that she had; she was not entirely disagreeable to look upon.

The girl lay in the glow of his light, surrounded on all sides by darkness. Martin imagined the light might be bothering her and turned the beam on the ceiling of the crypt. Enough light reflected off the white-washed stone so that he could still see her in detail.

A draft from the open crypt door rustled the lace on her sleeves. It did not startle Martin, nor the girl for that matter, but he suddenly felt like an intruder. With grave respect, he lowered the lid and left as quickly as he had come.

By the time he had returned home it was past midnight. He crept into bed beside the still form of his wife and lay staring at the pale ceiling above him.

What had he done? He had not even thought about looking for valuables in the girl's casket. He had only invaded her sanctuary to gawk at her; to look at her death as if she had been a painting—or worse, only a passing curiosity. Shame encroached upon him, replacing the excitement he'd known earlier that evening.

What in hell was I thinking? I must never do that again, he commanded himself. The thought repeated over and over again as he lay in the dark, trying desperately to sleep.

At breakfast he shook his head at the guilt that had assailed him before falling asleep. At lunch, he laughed at his solemn resolve to *never do that again.* By dinnertime, he wondered openly why he had left the girl's crypt so quickly. Sitting beside his wife, watching television that night, he passionately desired to return to the tombs. He wanted to see another face.

He did not go. Instead, he tried to sleep, but lay awake most of the night in anticipation of what he might find on his next venture into the Cities of the Dead.

He set out the very next night.

Twice, he opened crypts that had nothing but dust remaining in them. His third attempt was worth the effort of overcoming the complicated lock and seal on the crypt door. Inside a black coffin he found a man of considerably advanced age. The dead man's skin was much like the old woman's from that first night. But in contrast to her peaceful repose, this man's face appeared to be in pain. The jaw had dropped as the skin around it had first shriveled in the heat then broke apart. Although there were no other features that set it apart from the old woman, Martin felt certain this man was not resting in eternity. It worried him. He wondered just what sort of life the man had lived that would leave him in such a permanent state of vexation and torment.

He did not feel like an intruder that night. He felt helpless—unable to aid the man in his pain. After nearly an hour of watching the suffering man, Martin became aware of a palpable terror filling the crypt; as if the terror had flowed from the open maw of the dead corpse during the whole hour. Martin had not noticed it in the first moments of opening the coffin, but once it had filled the crypt with an overbearing presence he had to get out.

It required great strength of will to approach the open coffin and seal it shut. A chill ran through him as he secured the latches. The open jaw gaped at him each step of the way home. He dared not turn back, lest it reach from beyond the crypt and spew its maleficence over him.

He stayed away from the cemeteries for a week. But on the eighth day he found himself back over the crypt wall. He had to see more. Over the course of the next month he saw faces as calm as the old woman's, some younger than that first girl, many older, but each time he went back, he was looking for something new and remarkable. Some faces disgusted him and he fled from these. Others, just as grotesque, fascinated him, and he stood staring at them for hours. He studied their every detail. Questions overwhelmed him—whose body had this been? What type of person had looked out of those eyes? What sins lay upon its soul? There was so much he wanted to know.

"You're supposed to eat it, not stare at it." His wife sat opposite him at the table. "You haven't even picked up your fork."

Martin was not listening to her. He was thinking of a lady's face. But not one from inside a burial chamber. It had been the face of a lady at the car dealership that morning. There had been nothing remarkable about her. She had been the first live woman, however, that he had pictured as a corpse. Yes, he had thought as she walked into the showroom, she would find no peace in the grave. Her agitation and dissatisfaction with life were readily evident to Martin. It would carry over into the next world. He looked at her polished, tanned, and heavily made-up face and watched as it dried up before she could speak to him. Her high cheeks sank back against the shape of her skull and Martin had been shocked to hear her ask him a question.

"Do you sell any used models?" A clear, high, finishing school voice came out of her angst-ridden death mask.

Sickened with revulsion, Martin had barely been able to look her in the eye and respond.

He wondered over his revulsion all during dinner. Why had his illusion so disturbed him? It should have captivated him, like the others. None of the other faces of the dead had affected him in such a hideous manner.

"I'm speaking to you, Martin!" his wife picked sharply.

Speaking. Martin looked up at her and mumbled an apology.

As she upbraided him for his lack of etiquette, Martin was struck with an idea. Could his mind conjure the same illusion with his wife's face? Could he imagine her with a face from the grave? He was shocked at how little effort it took. Even as he contemplated doing it, her forehead began to tighten and her lips pulled back from her teeth as she was in the very act of speaking. For the first time in many years, Martin Broder could not take his eyes off his wife's appearance. A flash of memory hit him like lightning and he remembered how she had cut her forehead after falling in the shower. And there, in his vision of her death mask, as the hair thinned and retreated with the shrinking forehead, he could clearly see the half-inch white scar against the browned and desiccated skin.

"And what's that look for all of a sudden? Don't act as if you're suddenly interested in me. You sit there night after night, silent as the dead—you never say a word to me."

Martin nearly fell over as her words burned like fire in his soul. That was it! The woman in the showroom; he'd imagined her with the face of one of the dead, just as he was doing with his wife, but they had both been speaking. He had never seen one of the dead speak! And she was telling him *why*. He never spoke to them. In all that time he had never said a word in their presence. Martin's heart nearly stopped at the audacity of his epiphany.

He had been bothered more and more as to why he felt so drawn to see the dead. It made no sense to him. No matter how often he looked into their eyes, no matter how many times he studied every curve of their lifeless countenance, he felt drawn back for more. He had become an insatiable voyeur of death and he could not understand how it had come to be.

He could see it all now. They had been calling him. They wanted to communicate.

A creeping terror filled him as he pictured the gaping maw of that old man. He did not want to imagine what that tortured soul would want to say. Dread and loathing overcame Martin and he jumped to his feet, knocking over his chair.

"I won't listen!" He fled from the grotesque image of his surprised wife and ran into the night.

His flight through the foggy darkness could only end one way. He knew this. He knew it could never end any other way. The gates of Lafayette Cemetery Number One rose before him out of the mist. Martin shuddered.

With no resistance to his fate, he made his way to the crypt wall and stood eyeing it. Just on the other side—they were waiting. He would have to speak to one of them, and then the dead would speak back. His certainty of this was unshakable. Even as he understood it, he saw a glimmer of hope, the mere possibility of salvation. He would speak to one of them. But which one? He could choose. He was acting under very little self-will at that moment, but he could discern that this one choice had been left to him.

Trembling, Martin went over the crypt wall and entered the maze of tombs. He passed silently along the streets of the dead as if he too were a shade with an unsettled soul. He did not seek out a former victim of his grave robbing. He did not wish to converse with any corpse he had previously gazed upon. There was one tomb that he focused his attention on with deadly resolve. A tomb he had avoided ever since he'd become a pickpocket of the dearly departed.

He stopped before a plain, white crypt. Over the entrance he read the name: Martha Broder.

There was no longer any need for pretence. No discreet need to pick the lock. He no longer cared if any knew he had been there. He lifted a heavy iron flower stand and slammed it violently down upon the crypt's lock. The old, rusted lock and clasp twisted under the impact and broke in two. Martin pulled open the crypt door and stepped inside.

Opening the aged casket, Martin was not surprised to see that the old woman's remains were still recognizable, though they should have been turned to dust two decades before. But Martin knew better; she had been waiting.

He stood beside her—silent. He did not know what to say. He was terrified of what the dead would say in return. But if they had to say it, he wanted it to come from her.

"Mother," Martin could barely whisper enough to be heard. The corpse before him did not move.

Martin could hardly speak again. His voice froze. He could barely call to her. In the silence, he stared at her. There was nothing fascinating about her. She was simply dead.

"Mother!" Martin's tone grew impatient but her mouth remained shut.

He could no longer look upon her. There was nothing to be found in the faces of the dead. He had been bewitched by nothing; a chimera, a shade as empty of meaning as his own life. Martin could see how dead his life had become. Robbing the dead had stolen every shred of life from him that he had ever possessed. He had been sucked into the world of the dead simply because there was nothing anchoring him to the world of the living.

And robbing the dead was all that he had left. Without thinking, he turned back to his old ways. His mother had always worn the one item of value that she had ever owned; her grandmother's emerald ring. Reaching for it, he lifted his mother's right hand at the wrist and grasped the ring to slide it from her finger.

Martha Broder's fingers clamped down on her son's hand with ferocious strength. Her left hand reached up and clasped his shirt by the collar, dragging him down to her. Martin cried out, even as she hissed in his ear—

"Grave robber!"

"No, Mother!" Martin shrieked.

"It matters little that I was your mother. You chose the messenger, but the message remains the same; *as you have taken, so you shall be.*"

The caretakers of Lafayette Cemetery Number One were shaken at the sight that greeted them as the sun rose over old New Orleans. Never in their experience had they ever seen anything like it. By all accounts, it appeared that a man had scaled the walls and forced his way into an old woman's crypt. And after uncovering her body, the man had apparently taken hold of her shriveled hand and died of a heart attack. Some fancied he had loved this woman so much that he had died of a broken heart. But that sentiment was as preposterous as those who suggested that the man had not been holding her hand at all—that in fact the hand of the dead woman had been tightly clasped over the hand of her love. The only certainty that witnesses could agree to was the look of despair and desolate anguish on his face.

The Prophet

(*Danse Macabre 59*, Notturno)

Ingratitude is such an ugly word. It is an even uglier vice. I'd been routinely accused of it most of my life. But as ugly as ingratitude was in my life, it was monstrously worse to see it after my death. I'm ashamed of it. But it was the first response of my afterlife.

I must start with what I could remember.

My death, the details of which are not important nor is it socially acceptable to speak of them, was immediately preceded by the arrival of a ministering spirit who very quickly dressed me in a loose-fitting pajama like outfit and ushered me into my family's crypt. Ministering spirit sounds comforting enough but don't associate such a being with the phrase 'ministering to the sick' or a 'minister of the flock'. Think more along the lines of 'Minister of the State Health Board' or 'Minister of Death Procedures'.

I won't go so far as to suggest this ministering spirit was rude or unkind but there was a definite lack of concern for my welfare. After nearly shoving me into the stone tomb, the spirit mumbled a number of regulations with which I am sure I was expected to understand and comply.

"No leaving your crypt until the Sun has gone down and *all* daylight has left the sky. No disturbing a crypt unless its inhabitants have shown themselves of their own volition. No entering a crypt that is not your own…"

These were only a few of the endless regulations with which I had trouble keeping up. A large number of my friends were going to be sore to discover death had as many dos and don'ts as life.

The spirit instructed me in proper etiquette, which mostly consisted of another list of don'ts, generally dealing with what one did not say to a fellow inhabitant of the cemetery. If half of those restrictions were necessary then I was bunking down with some overly-sensitive souls who were just as apt to sweat the small stuff regardless of their vital signs.

And that was when the ingratitude set in. Just as soon as I had arrived, I'd been yanked, shoved, pressed, and hounded by the welcome wagon and I was just about sick of it. What right did this bureaucratic spirit have to take control of me and impose his Hoyle's rules of game play upon me? I might have been dead but I was no child. For all I knew, this government ghost was nothing more than a crackpot who did this without a shred of authority.

But my sin was ingratitude, not incredulity. I'm dancing around the truth a bit. The fact is, I knew this ministering spirit had every right to treat me like a raw recruit. I didn't need to see his credentials to be convinced he had all the authority he needed. I felt it in my bones, the most stable part of me that remained, that this spirit was legitimate, and I knew it was in my best interest to pay attention to what was being said.

By the time this minister of death was done I was happy to be left alone. His high-handedness had burned my dearly departed soul and I was tempted to break every rule that he'd just tried to impose on me. I felt as if I were seventeen-years-old again and my father had just delivered one of his redundant speeches on responsibility. If the crypt had been built with a bedroom window I would have climbed out of it and shimmied down a stone trellis and I would have been *gone*.

But even in death I was no longer a teenager. There had been enough years of maturity in my life to give me the strength to fight off such temptations. In lieu of rebellion, I chose to sit in the dark and complain in silence—the true mark of adulthood.

What a lousy way to be treated, I noted bitterly. My life had just come to an end, all of my hopes and dreams, all of my familial bonds—severed. Was it asking too much for a little sympathy? Shouldn't someone have been waiting to take my hand? Didn't I at least deserve a little humanity? Hadn't there been enough bureaucratic heartlessness in life?

As the sun rose on my first day in the tomb, I fell asleep to the soothing balm of my grievances. Death was not going to be terribly different from life.

I avoided the family members with whom I shared the crypt. They were only family in name. I had been close to none of them in life and I saw no reason to try and change that now that we were all dead. If life's little constants were going to be held over into the world of the dead, then I had no use for their outdated and boorish ways. I made it my goal to seek my own generation.

This proved to be more difficult than I had imagined it would be. I had died at a relatively young age—at least I liked to think I had still been young—and there were not many of my generation to find.

During the first few nights outside my crypt I discovered that only a few of my neighbors chose to leave their stone homes. Being new, I wasn't about to lie in solitude both day and night. I wanted to get out and see what I could of my new environment. I needn't have worried about my family. The older crowd was content to remain shut up in their caskets. I'm not speaking figuratively, of course. As their bodies shriveled and baked to dust, and as the caskets were busted up and removed to make way for the newly interred, these spirits were no longer bound by mortal remains. It was a matter of choice that held them in place.

I roamed free just as soon as the light left the sky each night.

I ran into a former classmate on just my third night. His name was Tyler. He had died while we were still in High School. The traffic report had said his blood-alcohol level had been off the charts. But I didn't mention it to him. As I said before, speaking of such things was considered to be in bad taste.

We had never been close friends in school and our meeting had been awkward enough to remind me of the fact. We smiled and shook hands. There was little to be said. I wondered if he was as relieved as I was when we parted ways. I'm pretty sure he was.

I found Roberta on the same night. We had once dated. I'd wanted more, she hadn't. Hers was the wiser choice. We would have been very wrong for each other as lifelong companions. But she had always remained a fair, though distant, friend.

As with Tyler, we did not speak of her death, and for once I was in favor of this rule. I had no idea what one says to a suicide. Better to ignore the subject for eternity. This restraint enabled us to speak freely. Roberta had always been easy to talk with.

"It's wonderful to see you." Her welcome embrace lasted for a heartbeat longer than expected; for though we had no more heartbeats, we both needed to feel as if we not only still had them but we could feel them in each other's breast.

"I'd forgotten you'd be here," I said. "It's nice to see a friendly face. This place is dead."

She laughed politely, though I knew right away she didn't approve of such humor. It was one of those reasons we would have been a miserable couple. I had always known I was funny and she had always known I was wrong to think it.

"Well, I knew that eventually you and so many others from our classroom days would begin to arrive. Have you seen Tyler?"

"Yeah, we talked," I answered too quickly. She read the exaggeration in my eyes but didn't challenge me.

"He was the first, you know. And Donnie Gilbeau. You knew Donnie." She wasn't looking at me as we walked between two rows of silent tombs, but I nodded as if she were. "It should make for a more interesting place when more of them arrive."

"There'll be fewer than you think." I hated to dash her hopes, but I equally hated to think of her pinning her hope on something that might never happen. I started to explain but she cut me off.

"I know all about the storm. And I'm aware that so many left the city and may never return. We saw Katrina firsthand, you know. And we've heard bits and pieces about the resulting exodus. I know full well the reality of the state of New Orleans. But I still hold on to a few dreams. They're made of stronger stuff than those dikes."

She was smiling as she said this. I looked away from her, not wanting to question such optimism. At the far end of the lane in which we walked, I saw a tall, thin spirit watching us. He had long white hair and an aged face that I felt was familiar, though I could not put a name to the face. His eyes, even at that distance, were easily discernable. They were full of sadness.

I watched him as we continued our approach. Whether or not it was because of our approach, he abruptly turned and bent low to enter a modest crypt. He vanished quickly. I did not think that Roberta had seen him.

She talked of her family. Not those still living, but those with whom she shared her crypt. I had never known any of them and so I silently listened as she told me their names and how well she got along with each of them. Roberta had always been kindhearted though a little simpleminded. Maybe the two went hand-in-hand.

As we came to the end of the lane, I glanced over at the crypt in which the tall spirit had disappeared. Instead of reading a marble stele full of names, I was surprised to see only one. I was even more surprised to see it was one I recognized.

"Roberta, look here." I stopped walking and faced the crypt. "Is that really him?"

"Teddy Oracle? Yes, it is." She took my hand and urged me to keep walking.

"That's really him?" I asked again. She pulled harder on my arm and I gave in. We kept going, turning to walk along the perimeter wall of vaults. She finally spoke.

"He doesn't like to be disturbed."

"But he does come out."

"Not if anyone is nearby."

"Yes, I suppose that makes sense."

Teddy Oracle had been the voice of our generation. After toiling in obscurity for decades as a blues guitarist in off road bars and honky-tonks he had finally been discovered by the youth of my generation when he joined up with a rock-and-roll band out of San Francisco. Wearing black leather pants and a white poet's shirt that matched his signature hip-length white hair, Teddy Oracle and the Establishment cranked out their hits to SRO stadiums from LA to London.

I hadn't been one of his biggest fans, but there had been a two or three-year span in which he had touched a chord in my young soul—a soul yearning for freedom from my parents and the workforce society I was just becoming a part of. Most of this resonance faded away once I'd begun to make a steady living. Then one day, as if overnight, I'd ceased to be at odds with my parents. My boss took their place as foil. Songwriters of a more refined genre gave voice to life's little woes. Teddy

Oracle became a nostalgic tune on a classic rock station. And whenever I was in my car, and heard Teddy's shaky voice warn "Livin' Ain't Worth Dyin' For" and "Losing's Just a Win Away", I'd ramp up the volume and sing till my chest hurt as if it all still meant something.

Roberta talked until I left her at her crypt. It was obvious I'd cheered her up. I had no illusions as to why. She wasn't the least interested in me as a former love. But for that night, I'd been a welcome relief to her boredom as well as a pleasant reminder of her past; a nostalgic tune on a classic rock station.

Over the next few weeks I met a few more friends from my school years. I even ran into my first office manager with whom I'd only worked under for six weeks before he retired and died in the same month. We had politely mourned his passing for two sober days before we shifted the office back into high gear. Once we did, no one had ever mentioned him again. I was embarrassed to discover he remembered me far more thoroughly than I'd remembered him. The fact was I'd nearly forgotten he had ever existed until I saw him sitting outside his tomb.

During those same weeks, I had caught a glimpse of Teddy Oracle on three separate occasions. Each time, I watched him haunt the lane alone outside his tomb. Each time, I watched him hide at the first sign of an approaching spirit.

Death, as we knew it, became routine. I ceased wandering the lanes in search of old friends. Having found Roberta, Tyler, and a few others, I felt no compulsion to speak with them regularly. I knew where they were, as they did me. We left each other alone for the same reasons we had never kept in contact those first few years out of school. We had been schoolmates, but that had been the extent of our common interests.

I still chose the night air over the confines of my tomb though I rarely wandered far from it. But when I did, I always ended up looking for Teddy Oracle. I discovered that it did not matter from which direction I approached him. Nor did it matter how slowly I made my way towards him. He always saw me coming, and he always slipped back inside his white-washed hiding place.

After we'd played this game on countless nights, I had finally grown tired of it. Ignoring house rules, I decided to try to speak with the old rock-and-roller. I didn't care if it offended him. Standing outside his tomb, I did my best to coax him outside.

"Mr. Oracle?" I called to him as firmly as I dared, my voice carrying far more than I wanted down the lane.

The dozen or so spirits who were moving about all stopped cold and stared rudely at me. I did my best not to notice them. "Mr. Oracle, I would like to talk with you."

Of course I had known just exactly what I was going to say to convince him to come out. But once I stood alone in front of his nameplate, and once I heard my voice echoing off the neighboring crypts, I couldn't remember any words I had planned. I grew nervous, worried that I'd say something stupid like "I'm a big fan", or "I loved your songs". He didn't come out, and I retreated just as soon as I honorably could.

It was my turn to hide in my crypt. And I did just that for I don't know how long. By then I'd forgotten just what it was I had hoped to gain from meeting him. I knew I wasn't just looking for an autograph, but beyond that I couldn't be certain of anything. After watching Teddy Oracle after my attempt to crash his private party, I became certain that I had committed a crime. I could see the effect my actions had on him; he came out less frequently, he darted back into his sanctuary more quickly. I felt awful. *Everyone* knew I had done this. *Everyone* made an effort to leave him alone all the more. I was pretty sure that if eggs had been available to my spectral neighbors they would have pelted my home with them.

When I looked at it in the right light I had to admit I wasn't surprised. So much of death had been a direct copy of life, so much of it had been just another way to look at life, that this was certainly in keeping with my living *modus operandi*. That death was a facsimile of life didn't mean we were getting a second chance. It was more like a rerun on television; we were allowed to see ourselves again, from a later, more enlightened vantage point. What had seemed funny wasn't always so funny anymore. What had seemed exciting was, in fact, just a bit more tawdry than we wanted to admit. In my case, I could see that my insensitivity had alienated yet another soul. I hoped to God my wife didn't hear about this. If and when she joined me in our marriage crypt, there'd be no dying with her.

If this had happened in life I would have made a deeper mess of it. I would have tried to repair the damage. I would have gone back to Teddy Oracle and banged on his door until he was forced to let me in. I would never have taken no for an answer. I might have even taken pride in that. Surely the man himself would approve.

But despite the inevitability of replaying life in this death, I determined to force a change. There had to be some reason beyond regret that we were allowed to see ourselves again. Maybe it was arrogance to imagine I could change who and what I had always been, but I just couldn't sit there and indulge my weaker self as I always had on that first go-around.

I left Teddy Oracle alone.

"You never came back."

I was shocked when he came to my tomb. So was everyone else. I could see spirits staring at us from all directions. I had not seen him approach, but I could imagine how his journey through the tombs must have turned heads. How his tall, long-haired spirit must have cut through the dark night like the beams from a laser-light show. What I could see, now that he was close enough for scrutiny, was that he stood with drooping shoulders, which formed the same shape as the long mustache that hung over the corners of his mouth. His hair, once the pride and focus of so many album covers and concert posters, was no longer the color of whole cream, nor did it look as silky as it always had. It more closely resembled white ashes now, paper-thin and frayed.

His eyebrows were bushier than they had been in the glory days. The mustache was still there, though it was too thin to hide the lines around his mouth that pinched it into a frown. Most striking of all, there was kindness in his eyes that had replaced the anger of his youth.

"You never came back." He said it again. I was too much in awe to make any kind of intelligent response. "I'm sorry I was so rude to you. It would have been a simple thing to answer the door."

It was still difficult to speak. Only now I was contemplating the fact that Teddy Oracle was apologizing to me for being rude. Death was supposed to be full of surprises, but this was pretty hard to believe.

"Do you know how many people knock on my door?" His eyes twinkled as he asked the question.

"Look, Mr. Oracle, I'm sorry. I just..." there were no words to explain away my behavior. I had quite blatantly disturbed a dead man's peace for the sake of his celebrity. You can't justify that with a mumbled apology.

"You're the first." I had mistaken the twinkle in his eye for anger. I saw right then he was only amused. "What's your name?"

"Bill, same as your rhythm guitarist's." I don't know how I'd remembered that or why I'd added it.

"Yeah? Let's hope you're a more intelligent conversationalist." He laughed as he started to walk away. A wave of his hand told me he wanted me to follow. "It hurt my pride at first, when I arrived here and no one came calling at my crypt. I knew my popularity had fallen off, but I had this idea that my death would bring about this resurgence, you know."

"Oh, it did." I caught up to him and fell into step beside him. "There were all sorts of tributes, retrospectives, that kind of thing. Much of it more genuine than the sham they put on for Ozzie."

"That's not what I meant, really. I just thought that a few of the souls around here would remember the old days. I had this feeling that everyone had just forgotten me."

I wanted to protest that such a thing was impossible but he cut me off.

"It wasn't like that. You see, the fact was, I was remembered. But I was out of place. It was the same reason I'd finally given up making music. For a season, I was acceptable, a voice crying in the wilderness of our tumultuous land. But as soon as it looked like we weren't going to go down in a nuclear hell, no one cared about our collective soul anymore. They didn't want me to remind them of it.

"And that's what's happening here. They remember me, and they don't like the memory. They think they've dodged the bullet. They aren't in a lake of fire, so they don't need to worry about it anymore, as if they ever really did. And they really don't want the crazy prophet to stand on the hill and cry out for repentance again."

"I doubt that," I thought about the former classmates I'd met, "this isn't exactly heaven. People look as miserable and bored here as they did in life."

"Yes, you're right, Bill. That's why they don't want me around. They're afraid I'll point that out, like I did when I had a guitar in my hands. I can see it in their eyes. This fear that I'll start making noise. Rock-and-roll the boat, right? So they stay away. The only ones who don't are the ones that fear me so much they think they need to drive me away. Only, I can't go anywhere anymore than they can. So they just do their best to keep me shut up."

"That's why you were avoiding me? You thought I was coming after you?"

"Nothing personal, I just learned to be careful."

"So why don't you?" We'd only just met, and the question was probably impertinent, but it felt like he was eager to talk. I was, after all, the only person in that entire graveyard willing to speak to him. "Why not crank up your guitar and wake the dead?"

His big smile told me he appreciated the pun.

"The same reason I quit all those years ago. Even when I was popular, and the crowds filled stadiums from Berlin to San Francisco, they never listened to me. They sang along, they roared with approval, but few of them ever allowed it to change them. They moved on to the next wave in music, and I became…"

"…a nostalgic tune on a classic rock station." I hadn't known the exact words he was about to say but I must have guessed pretty close. He stopped and nodded at me.

"And that leaves me with my own regrets, just like everyone else here. I don't think I was wrong to be the messenger. But I must have had the message wrong."

I wanted to argue with him. I wanted to assure him that he'd been right all along; he'd fought for our youth, he'd made us see there was more to life than just fitting the teeth into the cog, he had shown us we were better than our societal instinct. But even as I formed a defense for him, I remained silent. He could see my hesitance.

"I don't mean the words were wrong. It's just that when you're young, and you get a hold of something true, something *powerful*—" he stopped, working out just the right way to get his point across, "—there's a great tendency to wield it like a bully, to wave it around boldly. You can get a lot of people's attention by knocking them in the head but that's a good way to knock their heads off too."

"With all due respect, Mr. Oracle, you're wrong!" This time I did argue. "And you're wrong about these people here. They don't fear you; they're in awe of you. You were like Moses to them, man. If they're afraid of you it's because you aren't just a Rock-God from the past. You still are one! And now they're here, caught in some kind of mix-tape loop where they can replay their lives and they know they didn't listen to you. Or maybe they didn't listen to themselves and it tears them up to realize it. You said it all those years ago;

> *get out the cage*
> *get out the door*
> *livin' ain't worth*
> *dyin' for*"

"Spin the Leslie and cue the Hammond." The old rocker nodded in rhythm, his eyes closed as he allowed the silent memory to play in his head.

We had arrived at his tomb. It was the latest hour of the night. Darkness had filled in every crack of the stones around us. The last stain of light had long ago fled the scene. Few souls were still out. We still feared the witching hour. It was our nature. I liked to believe I was more rational than the next man but even I wanted to get back to my stone pad and lay low. I just hated to stop our conversation.

"You said it yourself," he opened his eyes and I knew the music had cut off in his head, "this isn't exactly heaven. And if you're right about all of this, if I was their Moses, then I led them here. Because even though I called for change and made them question their world, I never had the answer for that question. So they gave up. They ran off with the greed of the next decade. They never looked back. And they wound up here. With me smack in the middle of them. Maybe you're right. Some of them want me to write a new song. Something they can follow out of here. But before I could, there'd be too many others who would tear these tombs down and stone me with the debris."

He held out a slender hand. I looked at it and thought of all the guitar riffs I'd heard those fingers play, all the autographs signed, all of the times that hand had pointed a microphone at a stadium full of his disciples singing his own words back to him. It looked too small to have ever done such things. Too fragile. I reached out and shook it.

"Teddy, you know we had our own responsibility in this. You didn't have to have all the answers."

"It's always an honor to meet a fan," he cut me off, ignoring my words. "Thank you for knocking on my door. Thank you for remembering. After you've been here awhile, you'll begin to think it's possible I was right. You'll begin to understand why your friend Roberta is here, and Tyler too. When you figure out why you're here, you will know I was right. And when that happens, don't worry, I'll understand why you don't knock on my door."

He slipped into his crypt before I could argue. The old me—the *younger* me—would have pounded on his door and forced him to continue the argument. I walked away instead. The night air had grown cold and though I was not made of bone I could feel the chill in my marrow and I rushed back to the shelter of my grave.

About the Author:

Jason Phillip Reeser lives and writes in Louisiana, where he and his wife Jennifer raised five amazing children. If you would like to contact him, please write the editor@saintjamesinfirmarybooks.com.

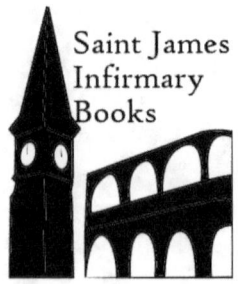

Saint James
Infirmary
Books

Dominique You, compatriot of Jean Lafitte and Hero of the Battle of New Orleans, is interred in Saint Louis Cemetery Number Two. Whether or not Jean Lafitte's attempt to find him was successful after scaling the wall vaults of Saint Louis Cemetery Number One in defiance of Monsieur le Maier is anyone's guess.
(photograph by Jennifer Reeser, 2012)

Author's Note:

It is with the deepest respect that I write of the cemeteries of New Orleans. I have often wondered—if members of my own family were buried within the walls of Saint Louis Number One or Saint Roch's Cemetery would I be offended if an author wrote such strange stories set in my families' resting place? It would depend, of course, on the stories. It is my hope and belief that the thirteen stories in this collection would meet with approval.

Of course, those who have family members in these cemeteries are already accustomed to the attention of tourists who tramp the lanes between the crypts, led by guides who spin wild tales of ghosts and voodoo rites and historical shenanigans that have little to do with real history. Some of the guides go out of their way to provide more level-headed and accurate stories for the sensation-seekers. Some of them do not. Be that as it may, those who see the Cities of the Dead as a place of rest for their loved ones are quite used to such public, oddball attention.

Though a few of these stories have plainly been written just for fun, most of them serve a purpose. Far from attempting to describe the afterlife, they in fact make an attempt to describe *this* life, *before* death interrupts it. Does this fact excuse me from accusations of exploiting sacred ground? I hope so, though that is not for me to say.

In New Orleans, the Cities of the Dead are constantly under attack from the elements, pollution, and the occasional sticky-fingered tourist who is looking for a souvenir. The only things I have ever taken with me from these cemeteries have been images captured on film, memories that will forever stay with me, and ideas which will forever haunt me. I pull out the photos whenever I need inspiration and am not near the city, the memories I cherish, the ideas haunt me even after I have molded them into stories.

Until you get the chance to walk the paths of the dead in the Crescent City yourself, I hope these little stories will be a worthy substitute. They are certainly more fanciful than any visit will be, though I cannot suggest they are more beautiful than a stroll through the real Cities of the Dead. But, perhaps, they just might leave a few ideas to haunt your thoughts for a little while.

Be sure to look for Jennifer Reeser's highly acclaimed poetry collection—

Sonnets from the Dark Lady and Other Poems

"I love these sculpted and energetic poems, full of drama and wit. Many of them are about the author's native New Orleans, which comes alive in them even for someone who, like myself, has never visited that storied city; others are set in the world common to us all, of love, heartbreak, and family. What they all have --- to borrow a phrase from one of them --- is 'that excess, that overflow / inherent in the bearing born of being.'"

–Michael Potemra
Literary Editor, *National Review*

"Having just finished Jennifer Reeser's third book, *Sonnets from the Dark Lady*, I'll just quote the Bard himself in his 20th Sonnet: She is 'the master mistress of my passion.' I think Shakespeare has summed up better than I could my feelings about this book. Buy it and better yet, memorize it."

–Timothy Murphy
Yale Scholar of the House in Poetry
author of <u>Mortal Stakes / Faint Thunder</u>

"Once again, Jennifer Reeser has graced us with a stunning collection of top-notch poetry in a remarkable assortment of styles, forms, and meters. Reeser's villanelles, couplets, quatrains, Sapphic stanzas, heptameters, dactyls, translations— and most prominently, her *tour de force* sonnet sequence in the voice of Shakespeare's Dark Lady—dazzle the reader with poetic rigor and luminous perception. In addition, their wide-ranging allusiveness brings back depth, maturity, and intelligence to a poetry world sorely in need of those things. Reeser is one of the most powerful and compelling voices in genuine poetry today."

– Joseph S. Salemi
Editor, *TRINACRIA*

Jennifer Reeser

SONNETS FROM THE
DARK LADY
AND OTHER POEMS

Available in print at online bookstores. Also
available for Amazon Kindle. For more
information, check out Saint James Infirmary
Books at saintjamesinfirmarybooks.com